Expanding Their Scope

The Women of T.H.E.T.A. Book 1: Abigail

By Elizabeth Borae

Dedication

Thanks Aunt Mad, for your suggestions and help! Without them, this story wouldn't have been written.

Chapters

CHAPTER 1

Calculations

Abigail

Lady Abigail St. Clair wrote like a mad man on the paper before her. The numbers and figures tumbled from her head faster than she could get them down.

"Lady Abigail," said Dr. Clinton Fiske from his desk across the room.

She popped a finger up. "One moment, please." *Can't lose this thread of thought.*

They were in his attic that he'd set up as an astronomy study. It was a large workspace with desks, bookcases, charts, telescopes, and all sorts of instruments for amateur astronomy. After reaching the bottom of the page, she rubbed her blackened fingers to ease the rawness. *Too much writing. But I must get it all down before it disappears from my mind.* She began writing again.

"Lady Abigail," Dr. Fiske repeated gently a few minutes later. "I hate to interrupt you, but aren't you attending an evening party tonight?"

"Uh-huh." She absently swiped a lock of straight, brown hair that fell from her bun and narrowed her gray eyes as she made a quick mental calculation.

"It's almost four," he said.

Abigail gasped, snapping her head up. She'd barely have time to prepare for the evening, and she hadn't completed her equations yet. "Thank you for informing me. I'll finish a few more lines and then leave."

His friend had left fifteen minutes earlier after making extensive use of Dr. Fiske's library. His musings on physics were interesting, and Abigail found their discussions assisted with her studies. Ten minutes later, she jumped from her chair. *I hate leaving. I want to play with numbers more.* "I'll return tomorrow, Dr. Fiske."

He nodded. "I'll be here."

"I've made real progress." She grinned. "I might be able to determine the orbit better."

"Excellent! I look forward to seeing your work when you've finished."

Dr. Fiske was of average height with steel-colored eyes and dark hair, a fit and healthy looking thirty-fivish-year-old man. The second son of a baron, he had made his way through medicine. A distant relative had left him an inheritance of a sizable property that allowed Dr. Fiske to establish himself as a landed gentleman again, but after several years, he quit the country to live in Bath. He still practiced medicine but spent a great deal of time in astronomy studies.

He was one of the few men who viewed her as something other than a good marriage prospect. Dr. Fiske interacted with her as an astronomy colleague. It was exhilarating. And a development that would not be well received by others.

Abigail threw on her bonnet and winced as she looked at her hands. *If Mama looks at my fingers...* She wasn't sure she could get all the ink out for the party.

She sighed, pulling her gloves over them and shrugged into her jacket. "Until tomorrow."

"Have a good evening," said Dr. Fiske.

Abigail ran down two flights of stairs and rushed out his back door, pulling her jacket a little tighter around her as she passed through his garden. It was the beginning of March and a bit chilly yet. She walked briskly down Dr. Fiske's street. Her town home was a ten-minute walk, and one she ordinarily enjoyed, for both she and Dr. Fiske lived in a fashionable district. She opted to travel up a steep side road, which was more secluded than she preferred but would cut a couple minutes off her trip.

Abigail prepared her mind for tonight's affair as she wound her way through the streets passing by homes, shops, and the Assembly Rooms. *At least I already know what I'm wearing. Mama will wonder why I'm coming in so late, especially when we have an engagement this evening.* Abigail turned onto the street where she lived, the landscape opening to a large grassy park slope on her left. The setting sun reflected off the pale yellow stone of the homes, giving them an orange cast.

I need to enter the house undetected.

******

Abigail slowly opened her front door and tiptoed inside. It was difficult to soften her footfalls on the tiled floor. She shut the door carefully and winced when it made a loud click.

"Lady—" the butler began.

She whirled around and put a finger to her lips, narrowing her eyes at him.

He ceased speaking but raised an eyebrow.

"I'm going to my room," she whispered.

"Your mother was looking for you," he whispered back.

She shut her eyes. Abigail was the only daughter of Michael St. Clair, Earl of Belden, and his wife, Mary Anne. Neither of her parents would approve of her doing research, especially as often as she did and going unattended to Dr. Fiske's home. Of course, there was usually some patient, colleague, or academic there when she went, and he had servants — it wasn't like they were ever alone. But Abigail still preferred to mask her comings and goings by calling on others before or after and being more mindful of the hour. *The numbers suck me in deeper every time.*

"Miss Yeatman is also waiting for you in the dawing room," the butler continued.

Why is Christiana here so late in the day? "I'll go to her directly."

Abigail tiptoed up the stairs to the drawing room and crept inside. Since Mama wasn't roaming the house, she'd likely be in her boudoir, which was down the hall.

"Finally!" Miss Christiana Yeatman exclaimed from her chair looking quite comfortable.

"Shhhhh!" Abigail hushed her as she crossed the room.

Christiana grinned, her huge honey-colored eyes dancing. "Why are we whispering?" she asked in a quieter tone.

"Mama doesn't know I just got in, and she'll have me by the hair for getting home so late," Abigail replied as she pulled her from the chair.

"What have you been doing?" Christiana asked. "Your hands are filthy."

"Writing," Abigail whispered as she opened the

drawing room door wider and poked her head out, checking for people. Abigail was still dragging Christiana as they started to scurry up the second flight of stairs.

"Abigail!" Mama called behind her.

Abigail cringed and turned, hiding her blackened hands behind her back.

"Where have you been, child?" Mama asked.

Abigail fought a scowl. *I'm twenty years of age, affianced, and have been in society for three years. Not that anyone can tell from the way I'm creeping around the house, afraid of being found out by Mama.* "I apologize. I lost track of the hour while calling on people."

Mama frowned. "You must hurry and change. You don't have much time."

Abigail curtsied. "Yes, Mama. Christiana is helping me prepare." She whirled and ran up the stairs, pulling Christiana behind her.

"Like a lady, Abigail," Mama said in an exasperated tone. "You sound like a herd of thundering elephants."

Abigail slowed down. Her mama was always telling her to do something like a lady. There were times when she felt like she was born into the wrong family. But she very much physically resembled her mother, so there was no question of that.

Christiana and Abigail went up one more flight of stairs to where Abigail's rooms were, styled in light green. She had an entire floor to herself — one of the advantages of being an only child.

Her lady's maid greeted them when they entered her dressing room. "Which gown did you decide on?" she asked.

Abigail eyed the dresses hanging off her massive wardrobe door.

"Do the pink." Christiana smiled coyly. "It's a little naughty."

Abigail chuckled. *Mama will hate it.* The pink gown had a very daring, tie front bodice, which she liked. Her mother would declare it looked like undergarments and then proceed to lecture her about looking like a proper lady. Again.

"I'd rather the pink as well, but we'll do the blue tonight." Abigail smirked. "I've vexed Mama enough already."

They began preparations. Abigail loved looking fashionable, and she wished to look well tonight because she'd be in the company of her betrothed, Walter Harding, The Earl of Darton.

"You must have something important to share since you waited all this time for me," Abigail said.

"I've met a man," Christiana announced, her voice filled with mirth.

Abigail snorted. "You're always meeting men." She turned and smiled at her friend.

Christiana's cheeks were flushed. Her dark tresses arranged in an attractive updo on the top of her head, and like Abigail, always fashionably dressed. Miss Christiana Yeatman was a beauty and had bunches of suitors of all stations ever since her very wealthy father had held a massive debutante ball for her four years ago. He had held a dinner last night for some of the lords and gentlemen with textile mills and insisted Christiana be in attendance. She'd suspected it was to show her off.

Christiana helped situate the dress Abigail's maid had just pulled over her head. "I've met THE man."

Abigail raised an eyebrow. "The man? Was he at your father's dinner party last night?"

"He was," Christiana replied. "Lord Thurston brought his mill foreman, Mr. Edgar Locke."

Abigail froze. "THE man is a foreman?"

Christiana smiled slyly. "He most certainly is."

This is not going to end well.

Stewards were very respectable, and a foreman hired from a nobleman's household such that Mr. Locke was, seemed to be emerging as a desirable counterpart in this new age of industry. Abigail wasn't sure how long that would last, for her society still didn't seem completely sold on trade, though the money brought in was impossible to ignore. But the positions of steward and foremen were viewed as servants — top shelf amongst servants and comfortably middling, but still not gentlemen.

"Well, tell me about him," Abigail said. "He must be very good looking."

Christiana exhaled and swooned onto Abigail's dressing room couch. "He's incredibly handsome — thick dark brown hair and such deep blue eyes that they're mesmerizing. I couldn't look away even if I wanted to. And he's just pleasant to be around." Christiana's voice was suddenly serious and earnest.

It wasn't a tone Abigail had heard her use describing other young men she'd courted. "Some of your other suitors were amiable."

Christiana shook her head. "This was different. I was completely at ease with him. Like I could be Christiana. Not Miss Yeatman, daughter of one of the wealthiest landowners on this end of England."

Abigail stared at her friend a moment. *I'm engaged and never felt that way in Lord Darton's company.* She assumed it would happen after they married and got to know one another better. It was a wonder Christiana felt it immediately with this Mr. Edgar Locke. "It's wonderful you're so happy with him, but how do you expect this to proceed? Your father will not approve."

Christiana hopped up and began pulling jewelry from Abigail's jewelry box. "I'm seeing Edgar tomorrow. We agreed to bump into one another at the mercantile."

Christiana held a necklace to Abigail's chest and frowned. "Too much."

"Please, be careful." Abigail shook her head. "You're already far too familiar with him. My mama rarely calls Papa by his first name."

Christiana shrugged. "My mama does. Mr. Arnold this, Mr. Arnold that. If she's not dearing him."

Abigail chuckled and then sobered. "How much do you know about Mr. Locke?"

"Honestly, not much, though he did share some personal tidbits with me. What jewelry did the advertisement show with this dress?"

"I believe pearls and hoops," Abigail replied. "Not much? Maybe you should make some inquiries first. Lord Thurston would be in a good position to tell you about his character since Mr. Locke works for him."

"Lord Thurston was with us half the night, and I know Edgar wouldn't hurt a fly." Christiana put the pearls around Abigail's neck.

Abigail gave her a look.

Christiana's eyes widened. "We're meeting in a public place."

Abigail sighed and hooked the earnings in her ears.

They finished, right on time. Abigail rose from her vanity chair and studied herself in the mirror. Her maid had managed to do something pleasing with her hair. The blue of her dress complemented her gray eyes well. The front was ordinary, but the back reminded her of a Grecian gown in how the different levels of fabric draped. It still had a tie-up back, though it was half-hidden, so Mama shouldn't say anything.

"You look beautiful," Christiana said. "Lord Darton will devour you."

Abigail grinned. "I can't imagine him devouring me. He's not that kind of man."

"Well, he should very much appreciate how well you look tonight and do whatever he does to show that appreciation," said Christiana.

Abigail hooked an arm through Christiana's. "I hope so, my dear friend. Let's find Mama before she goes into hysterics."

CHAPTER 2

Secrets

Walter

Walter Harding studied the floor plans of his estate home, Harding Court. They were laid before him on the large mahogany desk in the library of his townhome in Bath. He was a handsome man of twenty-five with blue-gray eyes and blond hair that had a good amount of volume on top. His intellect, countenance, and athletic build gave him an aura of stability, which combined with his good looks made him a respected and popular nobleman.

"Has the Dowager Lady Darton decided where she'd like her new quarters?" his steward asked, seated in front of his desk.

Walter sighed. "She has not, and it's not a topic I enjoy discussing with her."

His steward smiled faintly.

In a couple of months, Walter would be married to Lady Abigail St. Clare, which necessitated major alterations to his current living arrangements. The largest change was moving his mother, The Dowager Countess of Darton, from the family suite to other quarters.

They didn't lack the space for Harding Court was huge. He wasn't opposed to making improvements and fashioning things to her liking and comfort. His mother tended to be dramatic, so changes like these were always a headache, but she was the only family he had, and he endeavored to treat her with particular attention.

"I'll speak with my mother and move her to a decision. I know the staff requires time to make changes." Walter chuckled. "At least I have the money for it." He owned land that was home to several buildings, homes, and rooms in London.

His land agent, seated next to the steward, smiled. "Yes, your rentals this year did exceedingly well."

"Would you consider exploring building more units?" the land agent asked. "Some of the architectural plans bandied about are quite intriguing."

Walter nodded. "That sounds interesting, and I'll give it some thought. But perhaps after the wedding when Lady Abigail and I are settled."

"Bear in mind if you wait too long, you'll lose a good block of time for construction," his land agent said.

Walter drummed his fingers on the desk. "Draw up some ideas, and we'll discuss them. I'll come to Darton tomorrow and stay through Friday before leaving for London. I need to think, and that's difficult to do here."

This was the busiest time of year for him as he had state business he needed to keep taps on, and they collected the most revenue from those who rented rooms and homes for the London season during this period.

Lady Abigail had decided to do the Bath season instead of the London one this year, so Walter planned on being based here this spring. But he still had to be in

London frequently. Between his routine business affairs, planning a wedding, and getting the estate ready for a new mistress, Walter's stress levels were through the roof.

"I just wanted to confirm that the wedding will be on Lady Abigail's estate at Belden?" asked his steward.

Walter nodded. "Correct."

"Are there any further instructions on the engagement dinner you're holding the week before?" his steward asked.

Walter pressed his lips together, mulling that over. He hadn't a ton of time to think about that in any detail. "Have you been in contact with Lady Abigail?"

"I have, and she's been helpful." His steward smiled faintly again. "But seeing as you're the one hosting the festivities..."

Walter rubbed his face. "I know. I promise I'll speak with her and then get back to you on the final arrangements."

Lady Abigail wasn't ostentatious or particular, but she was well thought of in their society and carried herself with a great deal of poise and distinction. News of their engagement had been well received, and people believed them to be a good match. The engagement festivities needn't be showy, but they had to be right.

"Lord Manton would like to see some properties in London," his land agent said. "I thought you would want to personally handle that request."

"I do," Walter replied. Becoming better acquainted with Lord Manton could prove useful in the future, given his money, connections, and higher rank. "I'll write him directly."

He glanced at the large clock in the corner of the room and grimaced. "We'll have to bring this to a close. I have a dinner engagement this evening."

Walter stood and shook hands with the men. After they left, he headed towards his rooms. *I'm not looking forward to another evening party. I'd rather be with my telescope. Or with Dr. Fiske batting ideas around about planets and stars. At least I'll spend some time with Lady Abigail, and it's always pleasant chatting with her father.*

Just think about Lady Abigail.

******

After knocking, Walter's manservant stepped into his room just as Walter finished tying his cravat. "The Dowager said it was imperative that she speak with you. She's waiting in the drawing room, sir."

Walter exhaled. *Now?* He wasn't dressed, and they needed to leave soon. *What on earth could Mother possibly need to discuss right this moment?* "Inform her I'll be down shortly."

Walter surveyed himself in the mirror, trying to figure out what on his person he absolutely must attend to. He ran his fingers through his hair. *It's a little messier than usual but not unkempt looking.*

The light in his room was dimmer than usual. *Moon must be hiding.* His tired eyes stared back at him, as he had been up the entire night stargazing. It was hard to resist, especially when he was stressed and anxious. Stargazing made him feel like Father was still alive, and he had seemed to always know how to make things better.

Five minutes later, Walter entered the drawing room. The Dowager Lady Darton was a comely woman that struck an imposing figure. Dark hair, blue-gray eyes, and a substantial frame without being overweight, his mother sat on the couch as though she were queen, holding her cane like a scepter. *She's putting on a performance tonight. She'll be in rare form at the evening party.*

"Good evening, Mother." He kissed her cheek and took a seat alongside her. "If this will be a long discussion, can it wait until we return or tomorrow morning? We need to leave momentarily."

"No, this cannot wait," she boomed. "I need to discuss a grave and important matter before we go anywhere."

Walter drew his brows together. "What's wrong?" *Did someone die or something?*

"There are 'rumors' running rampant about Lady Abigail."

He raised an eyebrow. "I haven't heard any rumors."

She exhaled as though she were granting him the inestimable privilege of her patience with his ignorance and looked away. "The gossip mill has reported sighting Lady Abigail visiting the home of a single gentleman on a regular and frequent basis."

Walter blinked at his mother. "Lady Abigail? No, that can't be." He couldn't imagine the woman he'd been engaged to four months comporting herself in that manner. The wedding was in May.

"I've heard from the most reliable sources." She gave him a pointed look. "Note the plural."

Walter's stomach felt like lead. *I've always felt Lady Abigail was keeping a secret from me.* He had tried to dismiss it as nonsense. Lady Abigail was a beautiful woman, well-bred, and of the same social class as him. She was the perfect match.

But I have no plans of sharing her.

"Break the engagement," his mother commanded.

Walter nodded. "I will."

He rose, barely knowing where he was or what to do. *Now I really don't want to attend the evening party, and I certainly don't want to see Lady Abigail.* But it was too late to beg off. "I need to collect my things, and then we can leave."

Walter returned to his room and leaned on his end table for a moment. *I can't believe Lady Abigail would do this to me. Humiliate me in public.* His numbness faded as he narrowed his eyes, heat coursing through his body. *I'm good looking, have plenty of money, and a title. I treat her well. What more does she want?*

He snatched his things, extinguished the candle, and ran down the stairs.

"The Dowager is in the carriage already, sir," his butler said.

Walter nodded. *Lady Abigail never struck me as the kind of woman to have a secret liaison. There's more to her than meets the eye.* He scowled. *I wonder who the scoundrel is?* He climbed into the carriage.

His mother patted his knee. "You'll soon be over this. You're a rich, handsome man; you'll have no problems replacing Lady Abigail. She's not all that special."

Walter narrowed his eyes at her and then looked out the window as the carriage pulled off with a jolt. His heart twisted. He'd been looking forward to starting a family but would have to try anew with another lady and tread more carefully.

I can't break the engagement tonight, so I'll be civil with Lady Abigail and act as though nothing is amiss. But first thing tomorrow, I'm ending things. He clenched his jaw. *She'll not continue to make a fool of me.*

CHAPTER 3

The Letter

Abigail

Abigail moved amongst the guests at the evening party with ease, almost as though she were the hostess. She was well acquainted with everyone.

Mama approached her and smiled. "You look very well tonight, Abigail," she said quietly. "Perfection. A star as always." She gave Abigail an affectionate pat and walked away towards Papa.

Accomplished. Mama had spent a great deal of time making sure she was exactly that. Languages, dancing, extensive needlepoint, advanced piano lessons, the list went on. For the most part, Abigail didn't mind the education, and her parents were happy to provide it, which wasn't the sentiment in every family. She loved learning, especially science and mathematics, and enjoyed playing the piano.

Abigail also appreciated that her nobleman father, her excellent education, and good manners afforded her the opportunity to be well received. But she wished to spend more time and effort discussing and pursuing subjects that interested her. Not that all conversations were tedious, but she was bursting with excitement over the work that she had done with Dr. Fiske earlier, and she couldn't discuss that with anyone — at least not in this company.

Lord Darton entered the drawing room, looking very well in his blue evening coat with the longer tails. He had a pleasing height, sharp facial features, and a strong jawline.

Abigail smiled. *Here's something else I'm interested in.* "Lord Darton!" She walked over and took his arm. "How was your day?"

His smile looked forced. "I've had better."

"Whatever is the matter?" she asked.

He shook his head. "It's of no consequence. If you'll excuse me, I'd like to speak with Lord Thurston. I see him in the corner of the room."

Abigail pulled her arm from his. "Of course."

He gave her a short nod and crossed the room.

Abigail stared after him. *How odd.* Lord Darton wasn't effusive, but he was usually more welcoming than this. It was the first time she'd felt he didn't wish to be in her company. *Being with him was one of the few good things about attending this evening.* She exhaled and joined a group of ladies near the couch.

After a short time, they were called to the dining room, and Abigail was seated next to Lord Darton. "Did you take care of what you needed to discuss with Lord Thurston?"

"I did." His voice was hard, and he stared straight ahead, not meeting her eyes.

Abigail studied him. "I hope nothing is the matter—"

"It does not concern you," he said coldly.

Abigail's eyes widened. She was seldom ever spoken to in that manner, and never by him. She turned her attention to the gentleman seated on her other side.

Lord Darton ignored her the entire dinner.

Abigail's pulse quickened, her heart pounding. *I do not deserve to be treated in this manner.* On their way out of the dining room, she pulled him aside. "What is wrong?"

He scowled and took a step back. "Nothing."

Abigail grabbed his arm. "Don't walk away from me."

"Please refrain from touching me." Lord Darton shrugged her hand off him. "As a matter of fact, I'd prefer if you'd not engage me in conversation for the rest of the evening." He bowed curtly and stalked off.

Abigail's jaw dropped. She stared after him, breathing hard, and then asked the butler to fetch her things. *This is not to be born; I'll not take that behavior from him.* When the butler returned, Abigail instructed him to inform her parents that she was unwell and would return home early.

She threw herself into the carriage and willed her heart to calm down. *I can't believe how rude he was to me the entire night. How dare he...*

Why? He was all politeness and his usual ease to everyone else; she was the only one who received the icy treatment. Just two days ago, they had reviewed the final guest list for the wedding, and everything was fine. *What changed?*

I could call on him or write and inquire. She gritted her teeth. *No. I won't chase him as though I were supplicant for his favor. He may be Lord Darton, one of the most eligible gentlemen in the county, but I'm Lady Abigail St. Clare. Equally excellent, and I'm not to be spoken to or treated in such a manner.*

She looked out the carriage window. *Stars. I want the stars. They'll set me at ease.*

But there were none to be had tonight. Even the moon hid its illumination from Abigail.

******

Walter

Walter sat in the drawing room of Lady Abigail's home the next morning during calling hours. He'd always preferred the St. Clare's drawing room to many others. It had a simple and clean but high-born taste that Walter appreciated. Two pictures instead of ten. White walls instead of some ghastly color and busy patterns. Accents in gold, but there weren't too many of them, and they were tastefully done. There wasn't a profusion of furniture and knick-knacks, and what was there was of excellent quality. This home was fashioned much the way Harding Court was styled. That observation had given Walter confidence that Lady Abigail would have been comfortable in his home and as Lady of his estate.

He set his jaw. *But she'll not be Lady of my estate if she's someone else's lady.* As angry as he was with her, she had looked exceptional last night and seemed genuinely perplexed as to why he hadn't wanted anything to do with her. His plan to act as though nothing were wrong went awry. He couldn't stand to be near her.

He exhaled. *Oddly, there's a part of me that's upset to let Lady Abigail go, even with her behavior.* But it wasn't extraordinary to desire a wife that would be faithful. He had heard of other couples who had secret partners, and he refused to have that kind of marriage. While he felt Lady Abigail wasn't head in the clouds in love with him, he had assumed she'd be loyal. It had seemed in keeping with her nature. *But there was no denial of the facts. It's of no matter; I'll be done with her shortly and move on from this debacle of a relationship.*

The butler returned and bowed low. "I apologize, sir, but Lady Abigail will not receive you today."

Walter raised an eyebrow. *Marvelous show, Lady Abigail.* He smirked. *I didn't want to see her anyway.* He handed the butler a letter. "Would you ensure this is delivered directly into her hands?"

Abigail

Abigail was in her room that she used for correspondence and other studies when the butler handed her a letter. She was surprised for the butler seldom came to her floor and usually gave her letters to her maid to deliver.

Abigail's eyes widened as she read the contents. "What is the meaning of this?" she exclaimed. "Of all the—" She flew out of her chair. "Papa! Papa!" she yelled, racing down two flights of stairs.

Mama rushed out of her boudoir. "Abigail, please! Lower your tones. What's wrong?"

Abigail thrust the letter at her.

Mama began reading, her eyes widening. "Belden! Belden!" she exclaimed, running down the stairs to the ground floor.

Abigail thundered after her.

Papa appeared in the hallway, and Mama shoved the letter at him. "You must read this."

A moment later, he set his jaw and told them to follow him to the library, shutting the door behind him. "Abigail, what kind of resolution do you seek?" Papa asked quietly.

She wrinkled her brow. "What do you mean?"

"When I set things straight, I'd like some kind of goal," Papa replied. "Do you desire to save your engagement? Or is this strictly a matter of clearing your name?"

"The latter." She crossed her arms. "At this moment, I don't care to be engaged to Lord Darton, though my feelings may soften once my anger subsides."

He nodded. "I'll handle this immediately."

Mama's face dissolved into its usual serene expression after Papa left the library. "Your father will take care of everything."

She asked Abigail to accompany her to the boudoir. Once there, Mama patted the seat next to her on the couch.

"How are you?" She asked gently after Abigail sat down. "Were you in love with Lord Darton?"

Abigail widened her eyes. "No, I can't say that I was. I found him very agreeable, grew to like him, and we were well-matched. I was prepared to enter a good marriage and content with that."

Mama studied her. "Hmm."

"Why do you ask?"

"I'm attempting to ascertain the extent of harm done."

Abigail's jaw dropped. "The harm is incredible!" she exclaimed. "If his accusations are made public, my reputation will be destroyed, making a good match impossible."

"Yes, and that's why your father has taken immediate action. But if this destroyed your heart, that kind of damage could be incurable."

Abigail stared at her mama. *I've never heard her speak like this before.* "It's nothing like that. I'm quite astonished you'd even think in such a manner."

Mama chuckled. "That doesn't surprise me." She paused. "While I wish Lord Darton had done this in a different way, perhaps it's best that you not wed him."

"Why would you say that?" Abigail cried out.

Mama closed her eyes and patted Abigail's hand. "Parlor voice, dear. You must moderate your tones. Perhaps we should bring the elocutionist back here."

Abigail closed her eyes and shook her head.

"I'd rather you marry someone you loved," Mama said. "And he should prize you."

"Of course, I'd prefer that," said Abigail. "But we must be sensible."

Mama exhaled. "Of course, we should."

Abigail stared at her mother. *In the last twenty-four hours, I've seen those closest to me morph before my eyes.*

"Life isn't a math equation, my child." Mama stood. "We must show we're not ashamed because there's nothing to be ashamed of. Least of all you."

"Thank you." Abigail watched Mama cross the room. "You were in love with Papa?"

"Of course. I still am." Mama grinned. "And he still treats me as though I were a princess."

Abigail smiled as Mama left the room. She had never thought of her parents as being in love. They had a good marriage and were faithful to one another. But Mama had spoken of a far deeper attachment. She'd have to observe them more closely.

Her smile faded. In the meantime, *I'll need to engage in some societal warfare to win the battle for my reputation.*

The butler informed her that Miss Christiana had arrived, and Abigail met her in the entranceway.

She rushed to Abigail and gave her a huge hug. "I ran here as soon as I heard. How are you?"

"The news has spread?" Abigail frowned. "He was here scarce an hour ago."

"It's all over the streets," Christiana said. "Knowing the Dowager Lady Darton, she probably has her servants proclaiming shame from the rooftops."

Abigail groaned. "And what were you doing in the streets?"

Christiana gave her a sly smile.

Abigail shook her head. "The foreman? I thought you two were to stay in the store? In public?"

"Come. I'll share. Will we be safe in the morning room?"

Abigail nodded. "Father is departing to take care of

matters, if he hasn't left already, and I believe mother will return to her sitting room."

Christiana pulled her into the morning room, and the two sat next to one another on the bay window seat.

"We met in the shop," Christiana said quietly. "But decided to leave, as it would look suspicious after a while, and we wanted to be in one another's company longer. I left first, he followed, and we ran into one another in the park. We were still very public."

"Please, be careful," Abigail said. "You know how people talk. I wouldn't want the same thing to happen to your reputation that is occurring with mine."

"We're trying to be cautious, he especially. He expressed concern for my reputation if we continued meeting one another in such a manner." Christiana gave Abigail a wry smile. "I'm the reckless one."

At least he seems concerned for her well-being. And if he was more cautious by nature, he may be a good person for Christiana, who tended to be impulsive and strong-willed. "What is he like upon closer acquaintance?" Abigail asked.

Christiana smiled. "Edgar is industrious; he works very long days at the mill. He's brilliant. I have no doubt a great deal of Lord Thurston's success is due to Edgar."

Abigail raised an eyebrow. That wasn't to be taken lightly. Lord Thurston's mill was one of the most successful in the country. If that was partially Mr. Locke's doing, then he was a very able young man indeed.

Christiana's eyes grew soft. "He's very caring."

Abigail gave her friend a smile. "Then I'm glad for you to have met him. But I'm still concerned about how this will move forward."

Christiana stared at her a moment, her face uncharacteristically blank. "Are you against this?"

"Not in theory, but there are practical concerns and important issues to consider."

Christiana squeezed Abigail's hand. "You're a good friend. I understand your concerns, and to be honest, he has expressed them too. I promise I'll be careful."

Abigail nodded. *That's another point in his favor.* "Also promise that you'll keep me informed of what's going on. Someone should know what's occurring."

Christiana nodded. "Of course." She grinned. "I love talking about Edgar. It's absolute torture that I can't speak of him openly and show him off—"

Abigail laughed.

CHAPTER 4

A Gross Mistake

Walter

Two weeks after Walter had broken his engagement with Lady Abigail, he was walking through Dr. Fiske's very attractive garden whistling. It was tidy and neat — much like the owner himself. *Now I can relax.*

Besides the intense emotions he'd already been experiencing, Lord Belden had paid him a visit before he'd left for Darton. Walter didn't know why he hadn't anticipated that; in hindsight, that had been rather stupid of him. There wasn't much substantial evidence Lady Abigail's father could put forth to refute the allegations other than his vehemence that she wasn't in another relationship. Things got rather ugly, especially after his mother inserted herself into the discussion. Walter was ready to run away after that.

But now he was back, and he could always lose himself in astronomy fascinations with Dr. Fiske, who was good company and mentally stimulating. He also provided tasty food and drink, which was unusual in the home of a single gentleman in town. Walter walked into Dr. Fiske's house through the rear entrance and entered his study.

"Hello there, Harding." Dr. Fiske looked up from some papers on his desk. "You're here early. A couple colleagues of mine just left. It's a shame you missed them."

"Afternoon, Dr. Fiske," Walter said. "Hopefully, I can meet them another time. Just returned from Darton and figured I'd head straight here. I need to take my mind off things."

Dr. Fiske grimaced. "I can imagine. But usually, Darton gives you a peaceful frame of mind."

"Ordinarily, it's a welcome reprieve after the busyness of London and the social merry-go-round here in Bath. But I spent a good portion of the trip canceling engagement and wedding plans, so it did nothing for me this time."

"I'm sorry, Harding," Dr. Fiske said.

"I just can't believe she'd do something like that." Walter stopped short, surprised by the sound of footsteps rushing through the hall.

"Dr. Fiske! Dr. Fiske! I finished!" Lady Abigail ran into the study.

Walter's jaw dropped. *Lady Abigail? What is she doing here?*

"I finished the—" She looked towards Walter and snarled. "You!" She swiped a book off Dr. Fiske's desk and hurled it at him.

Walter dodged it, his eyes widening.

"Lady Abigail!" exclaimed Dr. Fiske.

"You louse!" She pitched another book.

Walter couldn't duck fast enough, so the corner grazed his forehead. "Ouch!"

"You lying—" She threw a third book. "Despicable—" She grabbed a fourth, but Dr. Fiske snatched it from her.

"That is enough!" he bellowed and dropped the book on his desk.

Walter rubbed his forehead. The only sound was Lady Abigail's labored breathing as they glowered at one another.

"I take it you two know each other," Dr. Fiske said dryly.

"Lord Darton is the one I told you about," Lady Abigail spat out. "The slanderer. Satan himself."

There are a few words I could call you, but I'm a gentleman.

Dr. Fiske looked between them. "I never made the connection—"

"What is she doing here?" Walter exploded, finally regaining his speech capabilities.

"Research," Dr. Fiske replied.

Walter snorted.

Lady Abigail reached towards another book.

"Abigail!" Dr. Fiske exclaimed.

She lowered her arm.

"I don't care for that attitude, Harding," said Dr. Fiske.

"She's a woman," Walter said. "What kind of research would she be doing?"

Lady Abigail's face clouded up. "Mama said you might have done me a favor by breaking our engagement, and now I see she's absolutely right.

"Done you a favor? When rumors have been circulating about you visiting men's houses—" Walter froze.

Men's houses. She was coming here. And there's no chance it was any kind of secret liaison. Dr. Fiske is the definition of a confirmed bachelor.

"Continue, oh brilliant one," she sneered. "What was that about the superiority of men's minds?"

"Lady Abigail," Dr. Fiske said, exasperated.

"I apologize." She crossed her arms. "I just hate to look at him right now."

Walter winced. *I've made a gross mistake.*

"That's unfortunate because I'd hoped someday the three of us could work together," Dr. Fiske said.

"What?!" Lady Abigail and Walter cried out.

"Harding, Lady Abigail is the finest mathematician I've seen, man or woman. You could definitely use her help." Dr. Fiske looked towards Lady Abigail. "And Harding has some exciting theories. If you assisted him with the mathematics, it could give you some notice."

Walter and Lady Abigail glared at one another again.

"I appreciate this might be an awkward situation," Dr. Fiske said.

Lady Abigail gave him a look.

Dr. Fiske sighed. "Could you two at least try?"

"I don't think you apprehend how much damage Lord Darton has done to my name," Lady Abigail countered. "I'll have to live with the effects of his slander—"

"It wasn't slander," Walter said. "I sincerely believed you were in the wrong."

She narrowed her eyes at him. "Regardless of intent—"

"Intent is important—"

"I have problems helping the very man who may have destroyed me," Lady Abigail finished.

"I'm sure you won't be destroyed—"

"Harding," Dr. Fiske gave him a warning look and then turned towards Lady Abigail, his face softening. "Please, promise me you'll at least consider it. You don't have to commit to anything right now."

She glared at Walter. "I'll consider it, but the likelihood of consent is slim."

"Fair enough," said Dr. Fiske. "I greatly appreciate you're open-minded enough not to shut the door."

Walter was about to comment on that, but Dr. Fiske

shot him another dagger look, so he snapped his mouth shut.

"Since I finished my work here today, I think I'll return home," said Lady Abigail. "I'll discuss my conclusions with you another time."

"I look forward to that discussion," said Dr. Fiske.

Lady Abigail gave Walter a cool look. "Lord Darton."

Walter bowed his head. "Lady Abigail, I wish you a good afternoon."

Lady Abigail snorted as she left the study.

"You know if we work together, we'll likely kill one another," Walter said.

"As long as you two produce something good before you do." Dr. Fiske stood. "Let's get to work."

CHAPTER 5

The Soirée

Abigail

Abigail shifted in her chair at a soirée two days later. "This is insufferable," she hissed to Mama.

Mama put a hand on her arm, a placid smile on her face as she looked towards the dance floor. "Dignity," she said. "Hold your head high. You're a lady with nothing to be ashamed of."

Abigail's dance card was blank. Hardly anyone would speak with her, though small groups looked in her direction as they were conversing.

Their hosts had two connected drawing rooms opened to a larger space for dancing and socializing and another room for refreshments. The grand staircase was grander than many in town and had a large area where guests could be greeted and gather. It was a wonderful setup, well devised for entertaining. Ordinarily, Abigail would have enjoyed tonight for her group of peers were present, and the space itself was lovely and comfortable. But tonight, enjoyment seemed beyond her reach.

Christiana crossed the room and reached out towards her. "Come, let's take a turn and go to the balcony for some air." She scowled. "It's a bit stuffy in here."

Abigail grinned as she grabbed Christiana's hand, and the two girls left the ballroom area arm in arm. As they left, Abigail overheard a snide remark about her escaping for a meet. She stopped short.

Christiana tugged on her. "Ignore them."

Abigail nodded, and the two walked out to a balcony corner. Abigail pulled her shawl around her tighter. The evenings were still chilly.

"Lady Abigail St. Clare," said a male voice behind her.

She made a face and then turned and curtsied. "Lord Kengsley."

Though she hated the sight of Osmond Beaumont, The Earl of Kengsley almost as much as Lord Darton, Lord Kengsley was very well connected and would inherit a marquisate. His speaking to her could improve her situation. He was easy on the eyes with a mop of curly brown hair and down-turned puppy dog eyes that he had perfected the art of using to procure his wishes.

"It's a pleasant evening. Wouldn't you agree?" Lord Kengsley asked.

From most people, that would've been an innocent enough question. But Lord Kengsley's tone held double implications not lost on Abigail, and he was the sort of man to put them there. That disposition was one of the many reasons why she dodged his pursuit of her two years ago.

"It is a lovely night," she replied. "Clear sky and bright moon."

He smirked. "Indeed. It seems you'll have ample time to enjoy them as you don't seem too engaged tonight."

Abigail narrowed her eyes. *And he calls himself a gentleman...* "Subtlety has never been one of your strong suits, has it?"

"Nor yours, Lady Abigail. Hence your current predicament. I'll let you ladies get back to your stargazing." He walked away, laughing.

"If I weren't a Lady—" started Abigail.

"I'm not," said Christiana. "Would you like me to relay a stronger message?"

Abigail chuckled. "You're close enough that you have to follow the rules too. What was said will suffice."

"I thought your father was to set things aright?" asked Christiana.

"Unfortunately, Father's intervention had little effect," Abigail replied. "It appears people rather believe the lies."

"I'm quite disappointed in Lord Darton," said Christiana. "I thought he was better than this. If I'd known he'd treat you in such a manner, I would have never encouraged you."

Abigail sighed. "It's not your fault. You couldn't have foreseen this." She bit her lip. "And the rumors aren't entirely untrue."

"What?" Christiana exclaimed.

Abigail took a deep breath. "I work with Dr. Fiske on astronomy."

Christiana blinked. "Work? You don't work."

"I'm afraid, in a manner of speaking, I do. I don't receive monetary compensation, of course, but I've been helping Dr. Fiske with mathematics equations and working on a project myself."

"Why have you never told me?" She sounded like Abigail had wounded her.

"I'm sorry, Christiana. It came on so gradually and became an arrangement, of sorts, before I even realized it was one. To be honest, things were clandestine because I was a woman engaged in science and math. It didn't occur to either one of us how it might look."

"That's most unlike you."

"I get my head in numbers and forget all kinds of things."

Christiana grinned. "Is this Dr. Fiske handsome?" she asked in a hushed voice.

"I suppose he's attractive — I've never looked at him like that before." Abigail shrugged. "He's just Dr. Fiske. I don't see him as a man, per se."

"Oh dear." Christiana chuckled. "I suppose that's going nowhere. I thought since Lord Darton was foolish enough to break off the engagement, Dr. Fiske would be worth a look since you both enjoy science so much."

"I never dreamed of combining science and marriage," said Abigail. "I'd reconciled myself to accepting I wouldn't be active in it like I am now. But I'd hoped Lord Darton would allow me to dabble."

Christiana raised an eyebrow. "Maybe you should consider Dr. Fiske?"

Abigail shook her head. "That would never work. He's... I'll have to introduce you to him. You'll see."

"Please do. I'm so intrigued. It's like a whole other side of you I'm seeing. Am I the only one who knows your secret?"

"Apparently, the whole town knows I see Dr. Fiske," Abigail replied wryly.

"Well, they know you see a man, but I don't think everyone knows who. And they think it's some secret liaison. I'm not sure what's worse for your reputation — the lies or the truth."

Abigail gave her a look.

Christiana reached for her. "I'm sorry, your secret is safe with me."

"Thank you. My parents know I sometimes call on him, but they don't know how frequently, or that I engage in research. Besides Dr. Fiske, only you and Lord Darton know."

"Lord Darton?" Her face reddened as it turned to thunder. "He knew, and he broke things off like this—"

"He didn't know until we ran into each other at Dr. Fiske's house after he broke our engagement."

"That must have been quite the meeting."

Abigail cleared her throat. "Lord Darton may have been hit in the head with a book."

Christiana threw her head back in laughter. "Good! I'm glad you let him have it. Knock him off his high horse and show him what you're made of." She glanced towards the house. "Come, let's return. We've been gone long enough, and it's cold."

As the two walked back inside, Abigail collided with a very solid body. "Ompf!" she exclaimed.

"I beg your pardon," Lord Darton said as he steadied her.

The area became quiet, heads turning towards them. The bright white open space felt like a tiny cupboard as Abigail and Lord Darton stared at one another a moment.

"Lady Abigail," Lord Darton said, giving her a short bow.

"I'm surprised you're even speaking to her." Lady Edith Beaumont's shrill voice cut through the hall.

Abigail cringed. Besides Lady Edith's voice grating on her being, the woman had also distinguished herself as the biggest gossip in their set in the single year she'd been in society. She was Lord Kengsley's younger sister, so people tended to tread carefully with her, as she had the same powerful net of connections.

Lady Edith was a very pretty, young woman of nineteen with long strawberry blonde curls, deep brown eyes, and a porcelain complexion. Her features gave her an innocent appearance. After a year in her society, Abigail was convinced of the falsity of that impression.

Lady Edith stood next to Lord Darton. "I witnessed her scurrying away from Dr. Fiske's home myself." She raised an eyebrow at Abigail, a coy smile upon her lips.

Abigail narrowed her eyes at her. She'd always sensed that Lady Edith regarded her as competition, of sorts. It didn't surprise her that she reveled in her misfortunes; Abigail wondered if she had a hand in them.

Lord Darton's jaw looked rigid. "Lady Edith, since we're not in any way connected, I kindly ask that you allow me to determine with whom I can and cannot speak."

Abigail's jaw dropped before she remembered how unladylike that was and then snapped it back in place. *I wouldn't think he'd do something like that so decisively; he's a non-confrontational man.* And he did it on her behalf, which he should have done since some of this mess is his fault. But on the other hand, what Lady Edith said was probably true.

Lady Edith raised an eyebrow at him. "Hmm..." and walked away.

Garret Isham, The Marquess of Thurston, took her place and smirked at Lord Darton. "You dispatched of her in a hurry, Harding." He shot a broad smile towards Abigail. "Lady Abigail, if you require assistance rebuilding your excellent name, after my friend has completely botched things, I'd be happy to oblige you."

Abigail raised an eyebrow. "Thank you, Lord Thurston," she said evenly. "I'll bear that in mind." *It's like a never-ending parade of awkwardness tonight.*

She's always had mixed feelings towards Lord Darton's best friend, Lord Thurston. His unusual features gave him a dashing appearance — wavy dark auburn hair contrasting with bright sapphire blue eyes and prominent cheekbones. A powerfully built frame lent him the same solid presence as Lord Darton, and the two made an eye-catching and attention getting pair. Lord Thurston was a marquess, which should have made his offer flattering. But he had a self-assuredness that bordered on arrogance which made Abigail wary.

Abigail replayed his words in her mind and glared at Lord Darton. "He knows? You told him?"

Lord Darton shrugged. "The turn of events was too astonishing to keep to myself. I needed to confide in someone."

I suppose that's true enough. Abigail directed her attention back to Lord Thurston. "You cannot tell anyone. At least not yet."

Lord Thurston sobered. "Certainly, though I don't think it'll be a great issue."

Abigail, Lord Darton, and Christiana stared at him.

"That might have been a simple statement," Lord Thurston said.

Lord Darton shook his head and then directed his attention towards the ladies. "I'll escort you two back into the ballroom."

Christiana raised an eyebrow. "That's the least you can do."

She took his outstretched arm, and Abigail walked on the other side of him with Lord Thurston following behind.

******

Walter

Walter now realized how much harm the manner he broke off the engagement had caused. *Miss Christiana was absolutely correct — this is the very least I can do.* It was amazing that even though the allegations were true to an extent, they'd been twisted into something ugly. Even he had assumed something was untoward. It had never occurred to him to think otherwise.

As he walked into the drawing rooms again, his mother's eyes blazed at him from a small corner table where she'd been seated the whole evening with a couple of other ladies.

The foursome walked along the edge of the room, avoiding the lines of dancing couples on the floor. Walter handed Miss Christiana into a seat along the wall, and Lady Abigail sat alongside her. She looked lovely tonight. Her white dress with the tiny flowers on the sleeves and bodice was simple but elegant in the way it draped her body.

"Would you ladies like some refreshment?" he asked them.

"We would." Miss Christiana rattled off a long list of items and then looked towards Lady Abigail. "What do you require?"

The corners of her mouth quirked up, and she rattled off a different list that was just as long. Then two women looked expectantly at Walter.

Garret chuckled.

They're going to make me pay. I deserve that much. Walter nodded. "I'll return as quickly as possible with your requests."

"We thank you," said Miss Christiana.

Walter grabbed Garret's arm, and the two headed out of the rooms. He was glad Garret was here this evening. They were good friends when they had been children, as their estates weren't too far apart, but their years together in Cambridge were what made them as close as brothers.

"I didn't realize Lady Abigail had so much spirit," Garret said.

"You have no idea," Walter muttered as he touched his forehead.

"It increases her appeal." Garret grinned. "I thought her a good catch before, but now she's captivating."

Walter suppressed a scowl. *I have no right to be annoyed, and it's not as though Garret was wrong.* Those captivating qualities had been part of the reason why he'd asked to be introduced to Lady Abigail last spring when they had been in London. *But I was engaged to her just a couple of weeks before. He could be a little more discreet in his admiration.*

They entered the gentleman's room where the refreshments were set up. There was an impressive display of light eats and sweets, along with a large variety of punches and other wines. While Garret filled the drink requests, Walter got to work on the food, deep in thought as he tried to remember the treats they'd listed.

"Have you lost your senses?" hissed his mother.

Walter jumped. "Mother, what are you doing sneaking up on me like that?"

"What are you doing associating with that woman?" she asked in a harsh whisper.

"It's not what you think."

"Of course, it is."

"Mother, we need to discuss this when we're home," he said. "I promised them I'd return directly with these." He held up the tiny dessert plates. *I almost need a third one, they asked for so much stuff.*

His mother glared at him. "Make no mistake; we will discuss this."

Walter stared her down. She was his mother, but he was also a grown man, earl, and lord of his estate. *She need not speak to me as though I was a child that should be scolded, and especially not in public.*

His mother nodded and walked away.

"I don't envy you that conversation," Garret said behind him, somehow managing to hold two glasses of punch and simultaneously pop an apple slice into his mouth.

Walter sighed. *This night can't be over fast enough.* "Let's get back to the ladies. They'll think we've ditched them and have further cause to be upset with us."

Garret smirked. "Us? I think you did this all on your own. With perhaps a lot of help from your mother."

Walter gave him a look. "She has her faults, but she's an excellent woman overall."

Garret raised an eyebrow but remained quiet as they returned to the ballroom. He took the seat next to Lady Abigail and began conversing with her.

Walter fought a frown. *You gave her up, remember? Stop being irrational and fix this mess.*

He stood on the other side of Miss Christiana and remained near them for the remainder of the night.

CHAPTER 6

Cautions

Abigail

Abigail walked to Dr. Fiske's residence a couple days after the humiliating soiree. She had told Mama she was calling on friends, which seemed to satisfy her. Admittedly, Abigail chose a moment when Mama was preoccupied with another task, and it likely never occurred to her mother that she considered Dr. Fiske a friend. Her plan had been to call on Christiana first and bring her along, but Christiana was meeting with her foreman again in the park. She had walked Abigail part of the way and then peeled off.

Abigail really had intended to visit with accompaniment. There was no need to fan the flames. A chance meet with some of Dr. Fiske's friends earlier in the week was the only reason she'd managed to get escorts to his house the day she ran into Lord Darton. Abigail had lost a lot of time over the last couple of weeks and hoped continuing her work with Dr. Fiske would vindicate herself. It could destroy her place in this societal set since a so-called real lady shouldn't be doing things like this. But it would, at least, reveal in more precise detail what she'd been doing. Dr. Fiske had said her research was substantial enough to publish a notable paper.

She opened the rear door. "Hello!"

Dr. Fiske greeted her in the hall. "How are you?"

"As well as can be expected."

He nodded, his gaze softening. "Understandable." He paused. "Harding will be here shortly."

Abigail growled as she followed him into his study.

He gave her a sympathetic smile and sat in his desk chair. "I'm sorry about these circumstances. It never occurred to me that Harding was your intended, though, in hindsight, I should have put enough together to ask." He raised an eyebrow. "Neither one of you mentioned names or seemed excessively enthused. It almost seemed like a business arrangement."

Abigail sighed. "It's not your fault. And, yes, I suppose there's some truth in the lack of romance. But I still...do we have to work together? It's most awkward."

"If you find it very disagreeable, then no, I won't force you." He jumped up and walked to the window. "But I was excited for this collaboration. I think it'll be an excellent one if the two of you can find a way to reconcile." He paused. "I realize I'm asking a lot of you, for it appears Harding was horribly in the wrong."

A door opened and shut, and then Lord Darton walked into the study. "Good afternoon, Dr. Fiske." He bowed. "Lady Abigail."

She gave him a curt nod in return. "Lord Darton."

He exhaled. "Lady Abigail, I beg you to grant me a massive pardon. I've done you serious harm."

"You have," she said. "But what have you done to counteract that harm?"

"Not enough," he replied. "I'll work immediately to rectify the situation."

Abigail crossed her arms and glanced at Dr. Fiske.

He gave her a tiny shrug.

Abigail sighed. "You give me your word you'll do everything imaginable to build my reputation again?"

"I do, Lady Abigail," Lord Darton replied. "You have my word and deepest apologies."

She bit her lip. *Focus on my goals and not the man in front of me. If Dr. Fiske is correct in his judgment of how beneficial this partnership will be, ironically, Lord Darton may help me reach them.* "I suppose it does no good to hold a grudge. I accept your apology."

Dr. Fiske smiled and mouthed, "Thank you."

Abigail gave him a tiny smile back and then looked at Walter again. "I don't understand why you didn't speak to me before you acted. You heard a few rumors—"

"My mother assured me she had reports from the most reliable sources," Lord Darton said.

"That's even worse," Abigail cried out. "You ended our engagement in the worst possible manner because of your mother?"

Lord Darton narrowed his eyes. "I happen to have a great deal of respect for her."

Abigail raised an eyebrow. "To a fault, it would appear. Are you not a lord capable of directing your own matters?"

Dr. Fiske closed his eyes. "Lady Abigail."

Lord Darton's face turned bright pink as he clenched his jaw. "I'm perfectly capable of handling my affairs," he said. "And I'll remind you that her information wasn't incorrect. Had you been more capable and better directed your own affairs, you might not have exposed yourself to gossip and ridicule."

"Harding," Dr. Fiske said.

Abigail leaned in towards Lord Darton. "How dare you—"

"Enough!" Dr. Fiske exclaimed.

Abigail and Lord Darton looked at him.

"Since each knows the other partners with me, I'd like all of us to collaborate," Dr. Fiske said at a lower volume. "We'll accomplish more in less time."

Silence filled the room.

"Can you two, please, call a truce so we can be productive?" Dr. Fiske asked.

Lord Darton put his hands on his hips and nodded.

Abigail crossed her arms. "Fine."

"Good. Let's head to the attic." Dr. Fiske said. "How long can the two of you stay?"

"I can be here the night," replied Lord Walter.

"Mama knows I'm making calls, but I must be back for dinner," Lady Abigail said.

Lord Darton smirked. "Masterful direction of your affairs, Lady Abigail."

"Harding," Dr. Fiske said.

Abigail glared at Lord Darton's back.

"You'll be working on your mathematics then?" Dr. Fiske asked her.

"Yes," answered Abigail. "I'll have to telescope another evening." *That might be easier to do now that everyone knows I come here, and Lord Darton is here as well. His presence might be an advantage in that way. Probably the only way.*

The trio entered the attic. Despite how agitated she was, Abigail grinned when they walked into the star room. *I love this place. So much to do and discover, and I have the freedom to play with all kinds of numbers.*

"Abigail has been working on calculations for her minor planet sighting," Dr. Fiske said.

Lord Darton snapped his head towards her. "A minor planet?"

She raised an eyebrow. "Yes, indeed."

Dr. Fiske gave him a wry smile. "I find the way you discount the female sex rather inconsistent, Harding.

I'd think a man who gave so much store to his mother's opinions would be more accepting."

Abigail chuckled.

Lord Darton made a face. "I'm accepting. I agreed to work with Lady Abigail, did I not?"

"Ugh," Abigail mumbled. "And to think I almost married you."

Lord Darton scowled at her.

"You miss a great many opportunities for advancement by not embracing females in this sphere, Harding," said Dr. Fiske.

"It's not that I don't embrace it; it's just extraordinary." Lord Darton crossed his arms. "A minor planet is a big deal for a man, and to find it's my intended—"

Abigail gave him a look.

"Ex-intended," Lord Darton corrected. "—is surprising."

"Point well taken," said Dr. Fiske. "Harding has what we hope is a comet, Lady Abigail."

She nodded towards Lord Darton. "Well done."

"Thank you," he said.

"I wouldn't think you had that in you."

"Lady Abigail," Dr. Fiske said.

Lord Walter stared at her, blue eyes cracking with the intensity of lightning. "I'm capable of a great many things," he said, his voice deeper than usual.

Abigail flushed and looked away. *That was...nevermind what that was, it's no good to dwell on it.*

"Harding could use your mathematics assistance in determining its return and orbit," Dr. Fiske said.

Abigail chuckled. "Numbers never were his strong suit. What was that about your great capacity, Lord Darton?"

Why am I goading him like this?

Dr. Fiske sighed. "I thought you two said you were going to work together."

"We are," grumbled Lord Darton.

Dr. Fiske gave him a look. "Refraining from being upon one another's throat is not the same as working together."

Abigail looked at the ground. "I apologize for my behavior. I'll attempt to do better."

"As will I," Lord Darton said.

"Thank you." Dr. Fiske grinned. "Now let's see what we can achieve."

At least one person is happy. Abigail plopped into her chair. *How will I work with Lord Darton and keep myself from wanting to wring his neck?*

******

A few hours later, Abigail slid into her seat at the dinner table just in time, blinking at the sudden brightness of the room. Her parents tended to prefer softer colors, but this room was an exception with vibrant lemon yellow walls and deep red curtains. A small but elegant chandelier hung above the table.

Her papa raised an eyebrow.

"Good evening, Papa. Mama," she said breathlessly.

Abigail caught her reflection in the large, gilded mirror that hung above the fireplace and smoothed back some errant strands of hair. Once again, she barely had time to prepare properly for dinner after returning from Dr. Fiske's house late.

After they'd been eating a while, Papa asked, "What have you been doing with yourself today, Abigail?"

She popped a forkful of food into her mouth to buy a moment to think. "I called on Dr. Fiske. He has a new star chart."

Mama gaped at her. "I thought you were calling on friends?" she exclaimed.

Abigail looked at her plate. "He is a friend, and I called on Christiana first."

"Abigail!" Mama cried out.

"It really was my intention to bring Christiana with me," said Abigail. "And Lord Darton was at Dr. Fiske's house too."

Papa gave her a curious look.

"I know," Abigail said. "None of this makes sense."

"Now it just sounds tawdry," her mother grumbled.

"Tawdry?!" exclaimed Abigail. "How is it that?"

"It's just bizarre," her mother said, slapping butter on a piece of bread. "Have you taken complete leave of your senses? Am I going to have to hire a companion for you?"

Abigail rubbed her face.

Papa sighed. "Perhaps now isn't the best time for you to call upon Dr. Fiske," he said quietly.

Abigail's fork hit her plate with a clatter.

"Abigail, please!" Mama scolded.

"You cannot believe—"

"Of course not, Abigail," he replied. "But your reputation is still on the line because of these visits. You need to be careful."

Abigail's stomach turned, but she picked up her fork anyway.

"And then we can persuade Mama to postpone hiring a companion warden," he said.

Mama made a face. "Fine. But I think it'd be best if you set aside all your star tomfoolery for a while."

Abigail's appetite vanished. "What?"

"It makes you look a touch odd," said Mama.

"Odd?" Abigail's voice was high.

"Monitor your tone, and drop it an octave, Abigail," said Mama.

Count to five. Patience. Serenity...

"What young woman has such an avid interest in science?" Mama asked. "You're the perfect model of a young lady, and then there's that one odd thing. And what will you do with it once you marry?"

"I'll continue, of course," Abigail said. There's no way I'm giving it up.

"What husband would want you doing such things?" Mama asked.

Lord Darton. Abigail gave a tiny gasp.

"What is it, dear?" asked Mama.

Abigail gulped her water. "Nothing, Mama."

Based on his behavior today, Lord Darton would've probably allowed her to continue if they had married. He had been a boor in the beginning, but once they'd gotten used to the idea, he and Abigail had discussed ideas freely. It'd been one of the best conversations she'd ever had with him.

Now that was truly odd.

******

Abigail was at Christiana's home in town, attempting to teach Christiana a new duet. The Yeatman's Bath home was in the same fashionable square as Lord Darton's town home, and about a ten-minute walk for Abigail. Recent events and revelations had left Abigail feeling off-kilter, and she hoped some time with Christiana would help her forget her troubles for a bit.

The Yeatman's home itself was a good start for taking her mind off things. They had a more ornate taste in decorating than Abigail was used to. Lively wallpaper patterns, rich wall colors, busy tiled floors, statues, vases, and pictures everywhere to offer plenty of distractions. They managed to make the eclectic decor work well, and it complimented their more vibrant personalities.

"I was surprised Lord Darton put Lady Edith in her place at the soirée," Christiana said.

"I was too," said Abigail. "It's rather unlike him. But

it appears he's fully apprehended the harm he's caused by breaking off our engagement the way he did. He begged my pardon the other day and said he'd do whatever was necessary to assist me in restoring my reputation."

Christiana raised an eyebrow. "Did he now?"

Abigail nodded and then winced as Christiana hit a wrong note.

"He should do all those things," said Christiana. "I'm just surprised he's doing it quickly and without your insistence."

Abigail placed a hand over Christiana's fingers. "You're playing in the wrong key. Let's begin again."

A few minutes later, Christiana said, "Maybe he regrets more than wrecking your reputation."

Abigail's hand slipped, and she hit a wrong key.

"I daresay he's very sorry he broke things off with you now. Serves him right; he shouldn't have been so hasty." Christiana smiled slyly at Abigail. "If he begs you to come back to him, what will you say?"

Abigail snorted. "There's no possible way he's entertaining such thoughts. And if he does take complete leave of his senses and asks to court again, my answer will be a resounding no. I can't be married to a man that's so attached to his mother that he'll blindly destroy his wife the way he did."

"Well said." Christiana gave a firm nod as she hit another bad note. "This is going worse than usual, isn't it?"

Abigail laughed. "Where is your mind today?"

Christiana gave a dreamy sigh.

Abigail rolled her eyes. "I should have known. Are you meeting him again today?"

"We can't meet until Friday." She giggled. "It's odd courting a man who actually works."

Abigail chuckled. Mr. Locke reporting to work every day would set him far apart from any suitor either girl has had. The more industrious young noblemen took on a project or two to occupy themselves, and of course, estates don't run themselves. But there weren't many their age who had full charge of their estates yet. Lord Darton and Lord Thurston were two of the few, and they seemed to have a more active interest in the actual operations than most noblemen. The other men they'd courted lived a more leisurely lifestyle. And they had managed to steer clear of the ones who engaged in less suitable practices, such as gambling.

"Are you two in a courtship?" Abigail asked.

"No, not officially. But in my mind, we are, and I'm pretty sure he's not giving attention to any other woman."

Abigail smiled. "How can he when Miss Christiana Yeatman has set her sights on him? I'm sure he can attend to no one else."

"Christiana, you need to exercise more caution," Mrs. Yeatman's voice rang out from across the room.

The two girls froze, staring at one another, and then turned their heads towards Christiana's mother, Mrs. Bella Yeatman. In many ways, Mrs. Yeatman reminded Abigail of her mother — the same tranquil, genteel quality. However, Abigail believed Mrs. Yeatman was genuinely sedate and mild-mannered. Abigail was pretty sure her mother exercised an outstanding amount of self-control and possessed amazing acting abilities.

Christiana plastered on a smile. "Cautious about what, Mother? I'm sure I have no idea of what you're speaking."

"I'm speaking of Mr. Edgar Locke," replied Mrs. Yeatman.

Christiana paled as she exchanged glances with Abigail again and swallowed. "How much did you hear of our conversation?"

"The whole thing," her mother answered. "I came to see what all the racket was, just as Lady Abigail said she couldn't be attached to a man who's so easily led by his mother."

Abigail cringed. *Those words weren't meant for anyone's hearing other than Christiana.*

Mrs. Yeatman nodded towards her. "Right you are, my dear. Mr. Yeatman's ability to never be lead was what drew me to him."

Christiana snorted.

"Which brings me to another point—" Mrs. Yeatman sat on the large window seat by the piano. "Christiana, don't think your father and I ignorant of what's been happening. Your father will let you have your little bit of fun for a time—"

"Edgar is not just a little bit of fun!" Christiana exclaimed, her face bright red.

Mrs. Yeatman stared at Christiana for a moment. "Have you given serious consideration to where this could lead, and what it might do to Mr. Locke?"

"I'm not letting Father stop me from being with someone I care about," Christiana said tightly.

Abigail gazed at her friend. *Are her feelings as strong as this for Mr. Locke?*

"Your father has creative ways of doing things and is just as stubborn as you are," Mrs. Yeatman said. "He and his father dreamed of passing down a vast business, a great deal of land, and a title. Your marriage to a nobleman would finally make that dream materialize."

"Then I'm sorry to disappoint," said Christiana. "But marriage to Edgar would not endanger what Father has already established. Edgar is very talented. He might help Father expand."

"I don't doubt that, but bear in mind that if things end, he'll make sure Mr. Locke bears the brunt of the damage. Are you prepared to expose him to those dangers?"

Christiana inhaled sharply. "Why are you against us?"

Mrs. Yeatman stood. "At heart, I'm not. But you must live in the world, and that world includes your father."

Christiana stared down towards the piano keys.

"And despite whatever fine qualities Mr. Locke may have, he'll not be able to maintain the kind of living you know," her mother continued.

Christiana's eyes blazed. "I don't care if he doesn't have—"

"Be sensible, child," her mother snapped. "You'll very much care when it stares you in the face day after day, year after year. The fact you even made such a statement means you haven't given it any real thought at all. You must come to grips with reality, and make sure you completely understand what it is you're embarking on with this course of action."

Christiana sat in silence, not looking towards Abigail or her mother.

Mrs. Yeatman sighed. "I'll leave you girls alone. I'm sorry to intrude, and it was most rude of me to overhear your conversation. Have a good afternoon, Lady Abigail."

Abigail smiled weakly. "Good afternoon, Mrs. Yeatman."

Mrs. Yeatman left the room, and a heavy silence descended.

"You agree with her, don't you?" Christiana asked, her cheeks flushed and jaw set.

Abigail grimaced. "I suppose I do."

Christiana glared at her.

"I'm not necessarily saying to end your burgeoning courtship with Mr. Locke," Abigail said. "But your mother raised some excellent points about truly understanding what a life with him will be like and how different it'll be from everything you know. And she didn't even mention the complete change of society you'll likely have to undergo."

Christiana exhaled.

"If it makes you feel better, based on how you've described Mr. Locke, I'm sure he's thought of all those things." Abigail gave her a small smile to try to lighten the mood. "He might be having nightmares about trying to keep you in the manner to which you're accustomed."

Christiana chuckled. "I wouldn't do that. I know he's not my father. That's probably why I like him so much."

"There may still be things that would be an issue that you never imagined. Perhaps discussing what Mr. Locke's everyday life is like would be a good idea."

Christiana nodded. "That's an excellent thought."

CHAPTER 7

Marry Dr. Fiske?

Walter

"I can't believe you're speaking to that woman," Lady Darton said to Walter. They were in the library after dinner Tuesday.

He downed his drink. *I'm going to need another.* "Lady Abigail has done nothing wrong, Mother. How many times must I reiterate that?"

"Visiting a single gentleman all hours of the day on regular and frequent occasions is nothing wrong?"

Walter winced. "Of course, it sounds awful when you phrase it like that. But there's nothing improper occurring."

Lady Darton scoffed at him. "How do you know that?" She smirked. "Because she told you?"

Walter jumped up and walked towards the drinks. *I need something stronger.* He poured himself a whiskey.

"How do you know, Walter?" She repeated, sounding less sure of herself. "What information do you have?"

"What I know is I will not continue taking part in destroying a young woman's reputation, and I suggest you do the same," he replied as he sat back down.

His mother glared at him. "She's destroying her own reputation. She ought to marry the man."

Walter's whiskey went down the wrong way, and he choked. "Lady Abigail married to Dr. Fiske?"

"Absolutely. It's shameful for her to be carrying on in this manner—"

"Mother!"

"Our society has dropped young ladies on much less, Walter," his mother said icily.

He threw back the rest of his drink. *That's true.* "Lady Abigail will not marry Dr. Fiske."

"Dr. Fiske may not be good enough, in her mind, to marry—"

"I can assure you Lady Abigail holds Dr. Fiske in the highest esteem."

"That settles it. She should marry him, and then no one would care. He might not be exactly Lady Abigail's rank, but he's a gentleman, of sorts, and fine enough looking." She studied him. "You weren't entertaining thoughts of resuming your courtship with her, were you?"

Walter sighed. "No, Mother, no such idea had entered my head." *I'm not so inclined, and Lady Abigail would never have me now.*

******

Abigail

Abigail paced the parlor of Dr. Fiske's house Friday during calling hours. *The gossip mill never rests, and it's intent on turning me into chaff.* When Christiana had called upon her, Abigail had dragged her to Dr. Fiske's house. It didn't surprise her that Lord Darton was there already. Their eyes followed Abigail as she paced — Christiana from the bay window, Dr. Fiske from a chair, and Lord Darton stood in a corner.

At tea the day before, Lady Edith and a few other women had not so subtlety hinted to Abigail and her mother that she should wed Dr. Fiske. Abigail nearly had a breakdown of mind right then and there.

"I cannot marry Dr. Fiske," Abigail said. "The idea is preposterous."

"I quite agree," he said.

Dr. Fiske was a pleasant looking man, and if she wanted a husband who would let her pursue science, he was foremost one. But Dr. Fiske was... well, Dr. Fiske. She couldn't imagine being married to him. She couldn't imagine him being married at all; he was such an idiosyncratic gentleman.

Abigail glared at Lord Darton. "Why can't you control your mother better?"

He rolled his eyes. "She is my mother, and very much her own person." He smirked. "You have met the estimable, Dowager Countess Lady Darton, have you not?"

Abigail growled at him. His mother was rather intimidating, and Lady Darton had always been cool towards her. She hadn't worked out how to navigate the mother-daughter relationship with her. Of course, Lord Darton had decisively solved that problem for her.

"Why don't you marry Lord Darton?" Christiana grinned.

Abigail froze. "That's just as ridiculous as marrying Dr. Fiske."

Lord Darton glared at Abigail. "While I too agree the notion is impossible, I don't believe it's as ridiculous."

"I know I said it couldn't happen, but I'm still here," Dr. Fiske said, chuckling.

Lord Darton winced. "I apologize. I meant no discourtesy."

"I'm teasing, Harding. But I'll make one suggestion." Dr. Fiske paused. "You two may want to restart your courtship, even if you believe, at this time, marriage is impossible."

"What?!" Abigail and Lord Darton exclaimed.

Dr. Fiske held a hand up. "It might make the rumors die back, and you can say you've been calling on me. It'd be a stretch, and a few might not accept it. But it could work. And Lady Abigail, given the circumstances, the sooner you get something published, the better."

Abigail and Lord Darton stared at each other. Dismay was written all over Lord Darton's face, as Abigail knew it must be plastered on hers.

"I'm willing, if you are, Lady Abigail," he said. "I helped create this disaster, so if you think it'll help, I'll do it."

Abigail exhaled. *I can't believe I'm about to do this.* "Let's court again."

CHAPTER 8

Let the Games Begin

Walter

Walter and Garret were on their way to the St. Clare's residence Tuesday morning during calling hours. It was the last day of March and a fine one. Walter had decided he and Lady Abigail could begin their second courtship with a ride. Garret had felt an odd urge to drive, so they were in his barouche, and he had the reins, with his usual driver in the rear in case he grew bored of the notion as fast as he'd gotten it.

"I heard Lord Manton was investigating properties in London," asked Garret. "Might you be involved with that?"

Walter was surprised. "I am. How did you hear?"

"I had a visit from Lord Manton as well. He has some innovations that might benefit the mills. Some talk about starting a possible English Textile Alliance or some such."

"Your mills are already doing quite well. I'm surprised you're so interested."

Garret grinned. "I enjoy new toys."

Walter chuckled.

"But in all seriousness, I'd like to be on the forward edge of things. My father was one of the first to implement new automation, and it took him far. I want to continue that same line of thinking."

"Are you thinking of investing in what Lord Manton has to offer?" Walter asked.

"Yes, I already gave him funds to build a machine for me."

Walter raised an eyebrow. "You must have been quite impressed with what he showed you."

"I was," said Garret. "Though admittedly, I'm taking a big risk here. But the rewards will be great if this does what he purports it will."

"Which is?"

"More cloth in a larger variety of patterns in less time," Garret replied.

"That's a huge advantage. And if it doesn't?"

"I'm out of a lot of money." Garret smirked. "But my recommendation or not will carry a lot of weight, so it's in his best interest to make this work."

There was truth in that, but it made Walter uncomfortable to hear Garret speak of throwing his weight around. That kind of arrogance could bring a man low if he weren't careful.

Garret directed his barouche onto the street of Lady Abigail's home. "Enough about business, as I want some more details on this call at hand. I'm perplexed as to how you came to be courting Lady Abigail again."

Walter looked at him in surprise. "I told you the rumors weren't true in spirit and what was happening."

"I understand that, but then Lady Abigail has cause to hate you forever." Garret grinned. "How did you convince her to court you again since you made such a hash of it the first time?"

Walter scowled. "This is an attempt to assist her in rebuilding her reputation."

"Is that all?" Garret smirked.

Walter looked at him sharply. *He's the second person to question me on that.*

"Admit it," Garret said, stopping in front of her home. "Once you realized the error, you were sorry you let her go, were you not?"

"I was sorry my error brought such disaster to her reputation. But it's not as though I'm devastated not to be engaged to her."

However, after working with Lady Abigail at Dr. Fiske's house, he had to admit that he was more sorry than he'd ever been. He never realized how keen Lady Abigail's mind was. He knew she had some intelligence and education, but her memory and reasoning skills were quite extraordinary. And Dr. Fiske was correct; she was a phenomenal mathematician. Walter wasn't sure how she accomplished that without going to a university. It was a surprising and pleasant addition to her other qualities that had made Walter believe she was an excellent match to begin with.

"I wouldn't blame you if you were," said Garret. "Women don't come any finer than Lady Abigail. You seemed to have been favored with another chance. I recommend you not blow it."

Walter scowled. "You've frequently remarked on her excellence. It's a wonder you haven't ask to court her."

"It wasn't for lack of trying." Garret chuckled. "I've tested the waters and don't believe she'll have me."

I doubt he tried very hard, and Lady Abigail wouldn't settle for anything less. Walter knocked, and the men were shown into her drawing room, where she and her mother, Lady Belden, entered a couple of minutes later.

Her mother gave him a frosty smile. "Lord Darton, good morning. You just keep popping up."

Walter bowed low. "Lady Belden, you're a good and gracious hostess."

She raised an eyebrow and then beamed at Garret as she dropped into a low curtsy. "Lord Thurston, what a great pleasure to see you. You honor us with your presence."

She held her hands out, and Garret took them.

Lady Abigail smothered what sounded suspiciously like a laugh and smirked at Walter.

He exhaled. Garret was usually paid a fair amount of deference as a marquess, but Lady Belden was laying it on a little thick. *I did almost ruin her daughter. I should've expected it would take effort to get back into her good graces again.*

Garret smiled back. "A pleasure to see you as well, Lady Belden."

"It's excellent that you're here to call on my Abigail," Lady Belden said. "I'm so pleased to see how unswayed by public gossip and opinion you are."

At first, Walter winced. *But this may work in our favor.*

Garret glanced at Walter, and Walter made a 'continue' motion with his hands.

"I've always enjoyed Lady Abigail's company," Garret said. "We have the most delightful conversations."

"You're always welcome in our home, Lord Thurston," Lady Belden said.

Lady Abigail opened her mouth, but Walter shook his head and mouthed, "In a moment."

"Have a wonderful time," Lady Belden sang as she sailed out of the room.

"Doing what?" asked Lady Abigail.

"I told your mother we planned a ride," Garret replied. "Harding, you have some explaining to do, for Lady Belden now believes I'm calling on her daughter."

"I think it'd be best to let people keep guessing," Walter said.

"Excuse me?" asked Lady Abigail.

Garret raised an eyebrow at him.

"Lady Belden saw the two of us and assumed, for reasons that are perfectly understandable, that you're here to call on Lady Abigail," Walter explained. "I feel others will be less sure as to who's doing the calling. I say let's keep them guessing."

"Intriguing," said Lady Abigail. "But what good will that accomplish in the end?"

"It'll take the pressure off of us having to be in a serious courtship, as we can just be amongst one another as associates." Walter smirked. "We could even bring Dr. Fiske along."

Lady Abigail gave a full bellied laugh, her cheeks pink and gray eyes warm.

Walter felt like he was punched in the stomach. It's the first time he'd witnessed her in such a genuinely mirthful state, and it gobsmacked him.

Walter's smirk grew wider. "Perhaps Miss Christina can join us as well. That'll set the gossip wheel spinning."

Lady Abigail clutched her stomach, still laughing, and Garret joined in.

I'll have to find other ways to make her laugh like that. Walter tore his eyes from her. "I apologize if this puts you in an awkward position," he said to Garret. "I didn't discuss it with you, and you were accompanying me as a chaperon. You don't have to join this scheme if it jeopardizes other prospects."

"This sounds like more fun." Garret grinned. "Though I told you before, Lady Abigail, that I'm more than willing to help you rebuild your reputation. We can get rid of Harding entirely if you wish it."

Lady Abigail arched an eyebrow. "The current arrangement will suffice."

Garret laughed. "Ouch. You prefer the man who burned you to me."

Walter glared at him. He may have said he wasn't looking to court Lady Abigail particularly, but that didn't mean he wanted to be denigrated in front of her either. *There are times when I briefly wonder how he and I are best friends.*

Garret chuckled. "I'll cease, as you both appear to wish me dead. If I meet a young lady with whom I want to court, I'll exit this arrangement."

"That's absolutely fair," said Walter.

Lady Abigail stared at Walter a moment.

Walter raised an eyebrow at her. "Yes?"

She shook her head, the barest hint of pink appearing along her cheekbones. "Nothing. I may have more respect for you now."

"Let's do this ride, shall we?" He opened the door to the drawing room.

Lady Abigail was still staring towards him when *What is the matter with her?* He gave her a look. "Coming?"

She shook her head again, the hint of pink deepening. "Of course. Let the games begin."

******

Abigail

Three days later, on Friday, Abigail was just about to leave for Dr. Fiske's house when her maid entered her room. "Dr. Fiske and Lord Darton are here to see you."

"Thank you." *That's a surprise. Is there a problem?* Abigail met them in the entryway.

"Harding and I picked up the new journal and figured we'd fetch you on the way back since it's so close to time," said Dr. Fiske.

"Marvelous idea." She raised an eyebrow at Lord Darton. "Keep them guessing?"

Lord Darton smiled and tipped his hat towards her.

Abigail's stomach dropped, and she placed a hand over it. *Why did that gesture suddenly make him look so handsome?*

Dr. Fiske raised an eyebrow. "Keep who guessing?"

"Lord Darton can inform you while I gather my things," Abigail said and ran back to her room. She shut the door and leaned back against it for a moment, closing her eyes and exhaling.

I must get a hold of myself. This reaction to Lord Darton began when he had launched that new 'keep them guessing game'. *Just because I like his plan and the idea of playing with people's minds, doesn't mean I need to lose my senses over him.* It was a little gutsy and imaginative — something for which she wouldn't have pegged Lord Darton.

She had obviously felt affected by him before — his looks were hard to ignore. Abigail had consented to marry him once, and she wouldn't have done so to someone for whom she felt nothing. But this is the first time I'm experiencing a powerful attraction to him.

She shook her head. *This is ridiculous. I'm no longer engaged to Lord Darton, and this 'courtship' is barely genuine. I can't persist in reacting to him like this. He didn't get me this excited when we were courting earnestly before; why is this happening now?*

Fifteen minutes later, Abigail was seated across from Dr. Fiske and Lord Darton in his very fine and very open barouche. She had enjoyed many rides in it before and would have had an even more comfortable station than she had now if they had wed. Her family was wealthy, but Lord Darton's wealth was greater.

Her father owned properties in Bath like Lord Darton did in London, and the two men had enjoyed discussing business matters with one another. The St. Clare's country estate was beautiful and pleasant but relatively modest. That more modest country living allowed Lord Belden's already sizable annual income to be stretched even farther. He kept a house in Bath and usually rented out the best of rooms in London. Abigail had a fifteen thousand pound dowry that would ensure she was more than amply cared for in the event of her husband's death and provide extra funds for whatever projects or improvements they might like.

Abigail was unsure if her father and Lord Darton took their business chats back up after she and Lord Darton had resumed their courtship. Her mama was cool towards him, even after Abigail had told her they'd come to an understanding. She'd imagine it would take her papa some time to warm back up to him as well, though she knew Lord Darton had spoken with him at length after they had started courting again. While Lord Darton and Abigail wanted to keep everyone else guessing, they had decided it'd be best for their parents to be aware of their courtship.

Abigail closed her eyes and tilted her head towards the sun, enjoying its warmth on her face for a moment. It was the beginning of April, and today was one of the first days that felt warm. They were traveling a route that was fairly public and had already said hello to a few people.

She opened her eyes and smiled at Lord Darton. "Maximum exposure, I see, Lord Darton."

He chuckled. "Indeed, Lady Abigail."

Her stomach dropped again as her heart did a little dance. *I must control this.* She took a deep inhale.

Dr. Fiske grimaced. "I'm not sure I like this new scheme of yours. Didn't you two take note of the fact that my plan specifically left me out?"

Abigail laughed. "Come now, Dr. Fiske. I'll soon take it as an insult that you're so fastidiously refusing to have my name connected with yours in any way."

"No, indeed, Lady Abigail." Dr. Fiske actually colored. "You're a fine woman for sure—"

Abigail smiled. "I'm in jest, Dr. Fiske, and if you're very uncomfortable with the idea, we'll be more careful in the future."

"No, it's fine. Had I been more cautious to begin with, we wouldn't have this issue." He sighed. "It should have occurred to me that our arrangement would cause talk. It's a wonder your father hasn't spoken to me about it."

Abigail cleared her throat. "He wasn't completely aware of how often I visited, and he has spoken with me recently."

"That's not good, Lady Abigail," said Dr. Fiske. "Why haven't you told him?"

"My parents have their limits," Abigail explained. "They've already indulged my thirst for science and arithmetic far more than ordinary for a young lady. They wouldn't like me spending so much of my free time studying it, even Papa."

Dr. Fiske nodded and held the journal out towards her. "In line with that, I have some rather bad news. Take a look at page eleven."

Abigail's heart sank as she read. "I've been scooped."

"Yes, it appears someone has beaten us. And their minor planet name is much better than what we came up with." Dr. Fiske grinned. "We might need to be more creative."

Abigail exhaled. *Someone has beaten me to the discovery. Now what? I counted on that more than my courtship with Lord Darton to get me out of my predicament.*

"Take heart, Lady Abigail," Dr. Fiske said gently. "This happens. We just roll up our sleeves and try again. Don't forget your work with Lord Darton."

Abigail looked at the two men across from her. *My colleagues.* She gave a decisive nod. "Absolutely, now I have more time to dedicate to those equations."

I'll be working with Lord Darton even more than I am already. Her chest tightened. *It's like I can't stop myself from reacting to him now.* She glanced at Lord Darton, who was looking as composed as he could be.

The two stared at one another a moment before Abigail swallowed and looked away, her heart hammering.

CHAPTER 9

By My Side

Walter

Two days after the journal came out, Walter walked through Dr. Fiske's garden, reflecting on how much he had enjoyed himself in Bath before he had to travel to London again. He believed it was due to spending more time with Lady Abigail during the last month. His shifting feelings were surprising and made him uneasy because he was afraid Lady Abigail didn't share his sentiments.

Walter heard a sneeze as he entered the study.

"I was hoping you'd get here first," said Dr. Fiske from his chair, his nose red and eyes watery. He sneezed again and pulled out a well-used handkerchief.

"You look awful," Walter said.

Dr. Fiske gave him a look. "Thanks." He blew his nose. "I'll have to stay in my room and miss our last day of work together before you head to London. My brain is too foggy to be of much use anyway. I'm trusting you and Lady Abigail to behave yourselves."

Walter grinned. "I think you'll hear us before the bloodshed gets too great."

"Yes, but that's probably not the only way you two could misbehave now." Dr. Fiske smirked and rose from his chair. "I'll be in my room if you need anything."

Walter was surprised Dr. Fiske had detected his shift in feelings for Lady Abigail. He'd been a little jealous when Lady Abigail had joked with Dr. Fiske, and the two had mentioned how often they worked with one another. They clearly had a close relationship.

Walter knew nothing was there romantically, but Dr. Fiske still saw Lady Abigail more often than he did, and he suspected that was true even before he'd broken their engagement. Dr. Fiske was better friends with Lady Abigail as a fellow astronomer than Walter had ever been as her husband-to-be.

She walked into the study and stopped short as Walter rose from his chair.

"Where's Dr. Fiske?" she asked.

"He made his apologies, but he's unwell and decided it was best for everyone that he remains in his room." Walter paused. "It'll be just the two of us today. Is that agreeable to you?" *I'm excited for this, but she may not be.*

Lady Abigail shrugged. "Yes, that's fine."

His heart beat a little harder. "Good." He grinned. "I wasn't sure if you'd especially miss his company."

She gave him a look, and the two headed to the attic.

"This will give us a good opportunity to work together since my work with Dr. Fiske hit a snag," Lady Abigail remarked as the two made their way up the stairs.

They hadn't been able to work extensively together a couple of days ago, when Lady Abigail received the bad news, because she needed to finish equations for another project Dr. Fiske had. Today they had a much more in-depth discussion about what Walter was hoping to prove and how her equations and formulas could dovetail with it.

The two worked quietly for a while. Lady Abigail's desk was next to his, and the nearness made his heart race. Walter was finding it increasingly difficult not to steal looks at her. *Calm down.* He exhaled.

Lady Abigail peered at him. "Are you having trouble?"

Walter shook his head. *Maybe if I talk to her, that'll distract me and bring some of my giddy tension down.* "How came you to work with Dr. Fiske?" he asked. "That seems a very unlikely collaboration."

"Indeed," Lady Abigail said dryly.

Walter crossed his arms. "Like it or not, women don't usually participate in science and mathematics. My question was a reasonable one."

Lady Abigail studied him a moment. "From that angle, yes, I suppose it is." She laid her pen down. "Dr. Fiske was one of my tutors. Papa asked him to work with me after I had become bored with my general arithmetic education."

"That's an unusual request for a father to make on behalf of his daughter."

"I believe that compared to the usual requests, he was more pleased with this one."

Walter chuckled.

"Mama wasn't as happy because she felt my time could be better spent elsewhere, and she still feels my preoccupation with mathematics and science makes me look odd." Lady Abigail made a face. "But since Papa wanted to do it, she didn't brook much opposition."

"Your mother's sentiment strikes me as odd," said Walter. "You're the lady to which other women aspire."

Lady Abigail raised an eyebrow at him.

He winced. "Well, yes, recently there was a little snag in that." He cleared his throat. "But generally, your person is admired and sought after. I don't believe anyone feels you're preoccupied with stars and numbers."

Lady Abigail smirked. "Ah, but how much time do you spend in female circles, Lord Darton? You'll find the opinion of me, especially amongst the more traditional set, much less generous."

Walter nodded. *Mother would be part of that set, and she is rather harsh on Lady Abigail.* He frowned. *A woman as gifted in math as Lady Abigail is should be allowed to pursue it openly. It's a loss to everyone to block her.* "You have the training of one who's gone to university and studied mathematics there," he said.

She nodded. "I suspect that's what Dr. Fiske based his lessons on."

"You're outstanding, Lady Abigail. An excellent mathematician."

Lady Abigail seemed to regard him a moment. "Thank you, Lord Darton."

The two resumed working in silence for a time.

"How came you to work with Dr. Fiske?" she asked, looking up from her papers. "Obviously, it's less unusual for men to engage in these pursuits, but I was shocked to discover that the man I'd been engaged to was an amateur astronomer."

Walter chuckled, and then it faded as he gazed at her a moment. "It'd appear we didn't know one another very well at all."

Her gray eyes locked with his for a moment, and Walter's chest tightened, making it, once again, very hard to breathe.

Lady Abigail cleared her throat and looked away. "That appears to be true."

"I sat next to Dr. Fiske at a lecture one day and enjoyed my discussion with him," he explained. "So, I started calling on him regularly. It didn't take long to discover we were both fascinated with astronomy."

"Were you interested in it before you met Dr. Fiske?" Lady Abigail asked.

"Indeed, since I was a young boy," he replied. "My father and I spent many nights looking through his scope."

Lady Abigail's eyes softened. "I didn't know. Those must be wonderful memories."

A lump formed in Walter's throat. "They were, Lady Abigail," he said in a deeper voice. "They were."

A heavy silence descended upon the room.

"I'm sure he'd be proud that you kept on like this," Lady Abigail said gently.

Walter mustered a smile. "I can only hope." He chuckled. "He was a little easier to please than Mother."

"She doesn't approve of your stargazing?" asked Lady Abigail.

Walter pressed his lips together as he thought that over. "She used to do it with us, so I know she enjoys it on some level."

"I have a hard time imagining her engaged in such an activity."

"Mother has always been a reserved woman, at least much more so than Father. But she was a somewhat different person while he was alive." He drummed his fingers on the desk. "She's never discouraged me. Maybe she feels this is how I can keep a little bit of him around."

Lady Abigail stared off towards the window for a moment. "I'll help you keep him too, Lord Darton." She offered Walter a shy smile. "We'll do something that would've made him proud."

Warmth radiated through Walter's chest. "Thank you. With you working by my side, I believe we shall."

The two shared a smile, and then they worked for another couple hours, the comfortable quiet only broken by periodic questions. When they finished, Walter escorted Lady Abigail home in his carriage.

"I suppose I'll see you next week then," Lady Abigail said after he walked her to the front door. "Hopefully, Dr. Fiske will be recovered."

"Yes, hopefully," Walter replied. "But I won't be there. I'll be in London for a few weeks."

"Oh." Lady Abigail pressed her lips together and played with her hands for a moment. "Have a safe journey." She smiled, but it didn't quite reach her eyes.

"Thank you." *I'm going to miss her.* Walter tipped his hat. "Have a good evening, Lady Abigail," he said quietly.

"You as well."

They shared one last look, and Walter walked away. *I should have never ended our engagement. What could have been...*

******

Abigail

The next day, Abigail sighed and let her hand drop heavily on the keys creating a loud discordant clang. *My mind is just not on playing today.*

Mama poked her head into the drawing room. "Abigail, what on earth are you doing? Can you be a little gentler, please?"

"I'm sorry to disturb you, Mama."

"It's not so much disturbing me; let's try to be a little lighter, more ladylike."

Abigail closed her eyes. *Why can't I be a man? No, why can't I be the woman that I am?* She opened her eyes and plastered on a smile. "Yes, I'll do my best."

"Very good." She beamed at her and then shut the door.

Abigail shook her head. *I know Mama only speaks so because she cares for me and believes those things matter. In a way, it does, as recent history has borne out.* Abigail made a face. *But I don't feel like being bothered with the pretenses anymore.*

Lord Darton's blue-gray eyes floated in her mind's eye. *I put on no pretenses when I'm with him.* She tapped a key absently for a moment and then pulled the lid down before her mother returned to admonish her again.

Abigail stared off for a moment. *'With you working by my side, I believe we shall.'* When Lord Darton had said that, she could scarce draw breath. *Not working for him; working by his side, as though I'm his partner.* Her stomach somersaulted.

The door flew open, making Abigail jump.

Christiana burst in with hair flying, her face red and streaked with tears.

The butler followed on her heels. "Miss Yeatman," he called in.

Christiana was crying in her arms as Abigail stroked her head. "Whatever is the matter?"

"He thinks I'm ashamed of him," she sobbed.

Abigail wrinkled her brow. "Who?"

"Edgar," Christiana hiccupped out.

"Why would he think that?"

Christiana's sobbing intensified.

Abigail walked Christiana to the couch and then poured her a glass of water from the sideboard. "Here, drink," she said, handing her the glass. Abigail sat beside Christiana as she took a sip. "Now, tell me what happened,"

"Edgar wants to court me properly," Christiana said, a little more composed.

"What's wrong with that?" Abigail asked. "Other than the actual fact of courting you."

Christiana nodded. "Courting me properly is serious, and Father won't stand for that."

"What do you want to do?"

"Court in secret and then get married in Gretna Green or some other place equally far away," Christiana replied.

Abigail gawked at her. "You're serious?"

Christiana glared back. "I keep telling you I'm serious about Edgar—"

"That's not of what I'm speaking," she snapped. "Your plan. Is that seriously your plan?" Abigail asked sharply.

Christiana's large, honey-brown eyes grew very wide. "Yes."

Abigail launched herself from the couch and began pacing.

"Abigail?" Christiana asked.

She scowled. "No wonder Mr. Locke is angry with you. I'm upset, and we're not even courting."

Christiana shrank back into the couch.

"A secret courtship and elopement?"

"I don't see—"

"That's the problem, Christiana!" Abigail cried out. " You're twenty-two years old, and Mr. Locke is a grown man with a real position and serious responsibilities. He can't just run off with you!"

Christiana cringed.

"Even if he could, he doesn't sound like the kind of man that would want to treat you in that manner," Abigail said.

A heavy silence fell upon the room.

Calm down. Try to perform that serene act Mama has down to a science. Abigail exhaled. "I know you're not ashamed of him," she continued in a quieter voice. "But it sounds like Mr. Locke is ready to fight for you, and you need to decide if you're ready to stand by his side as he does."

Christiana swallowed. "That sounds so romantic the way you put it, but the reality isn't going to be as romantic, is it?"

"I don't even know what romance is anymore," Abigail replied with a sigh as she fell back onto the couch. "I find myself falling for a man who nearly destroyed my reputation and broke off our engagement— falling much harder for him than any man of my acquaintance, and far deeper than before."

Christiana gave her a soft smile. "So, the courtship is very real now, is it?"

Abigail gave her a sad smile. "More than it's ever been on my side, at least. I don't know about Lord Darton."

"I have a sense you needn't worry about that," said Christiana. "It's one of the reasons why I mentioned marriage in the first place when we were all at Dr. Fiske's home. It was a joke, of sorts, but at the same time sort of not."

What did she see? I'll have to inquire one day. "I believe you'll be much happier and satisfied with the course Mr. Locke is willing to take instead of yours," Abigail said. "You can be assured what you have is true and strong."

Christiana nodded, her face taking on a determined look. "I'm ready." She polished off her water. "Edgar and I will do this the right way. Together."

CHAPTER 10

Not Lost

Walter

Richard Jarvis, the Earl of Manton, walked around the room in one of Walter's properties in London. Lord Manton was a few years younger than Walter at twenty-one. His looks were arresting with dark hair and eyes and a tall build. Walter wasn't well acquainted with him, but on the few occasions when they were in one another's company Lord Manton had struck him as a somewhat fastidious young man. He would inherit a non-royal dukedom upon his father's death, and in the meantime, had assumed full responsibility for the family's estate at Manton.

Walter was happy for the added distraction because he found this trip to London difficult. He longed to be with Lady Abigail in Bath. He could telescope here, avail himself of informative talks, and purchase equipment in London, but it wasn't the same. *I could buy Lady Abigail a new spyglass or book. Or maybe a new protractor. That's hardly romantic. But I think she might appreciate one of those things rather than the flowers or chocolates I used to buy her.*

"This might do," Lord Manton said, snatching Walter from his musings.

Get back to the task at hand. "May I inquire after the purpose of the space?" Walter asked. "I could assist in finding something more suitable that's not the specifications you outlined."

"We're living in an exciting time for invention, especially with textiles," Lord Manton commented.

Walter raised an eyebrow. "Indeed. Are you looking to establish a mill then? This location might not be the best."

"Not a mill exactly. I'm acquainted with a man who has an improvement on the loom. But we need a larger space to build and test effectively."

Walter nodded. "Might I still suggest a more waterfront property? I'm assuming these looms will use steam technology?"

Lord Manton nodded. "The waterfront will be more expensive."

"Yes, mine are, but even if you don't need a full-fledged operational mill, you might find it advantageous to have a ready source of power for testing and display purposes," said Walter. "It'd be a shame to make this kind of investment and not have it do what you need."

Lord Manton mulled that over. "I like how you think. What do you mean by display purposes?"

"I'm sure you'd like to sell this technology if you haven't already," replied Walter. This could be the machinery in which Garret had invested. "Having something on display to show potential customers how it works might be worthwhile."

"Excellent notion. You seem to have a ready knowledge of selling machinery."

"I have a ready knowledge of selling property. I'd think some of the principles would be the same. It's easier to sell a property once the person is on it. I'd imagine the same is true with machinery— better to see it in action."

"Yes, absolutely. I've shown drawings, pictures, and samples of the finished products. But you're suggesting an actual working demonstration to put on permanent display." Lord Manton got a gleam in his eye. "Maybe building a mill isn't such a bad idea."

Walter stared at him. *He is an odd man.*

Lord Manton started pacing the room. "I'd like to see the waterfront properties if that can be done readily."

Walter nodded. "I have two I think you might like."

A little while later, they were standing in the middle of the second property.

"I think this one will do very well," Lord Manton said. "Not too large, but enough for an office and floor space to get a working mill going."

Walter's jaw dropped. "You're actually building a mill?"

Lord Richard grinned. "I think a tiny one would be novel. I could sell a whole package, a whole textile mill experience."

He is a very odd man.

Lord Manton studied Walter. "Do you sell only the city property, or do you have land more appropriate to farming?"

"I have property in Bath that could be rented and used for agriculture purposes, but not here in London," replied Walter.

Lord Manton nodded. "That's very good to know, and I have much to reflect on. I'll speak with a friend and see if he'll invest in this property with me. If I asked you to hold it, how soon would you need a definite answer?"

The men made the arrangements, and Walter walked him outside.

"You're very good at what you do, " said Lord Manton.

"Thank you. You have some interesting ideas yourself."

Lord Manton chuckled. "Could I contact you in the future to further some of those ideas?"

"Certainly." Walter wasn't sure what he was getting into, but if Lord Manton had the cash, he wasn't opposed to partaking.

******

Abigail

Dr. Fiske was having a 'dinner party' for the three of them Tuesday evening to celebrate Lord Darton's return from London. It had felt like an eternity to Abigail. She'd never missed him so much, even when they were engaged and apart during the winter.

She'd like to know if Lord Darton felt the same way. Abigail had been surprised and delighted to receive his letters while he was away. They were different from the ones they'd exchanged the first time they'd courted. Their correspondence was much more personable now, and since they shared a love for astronomy, more interesting. Abigail sensed he wasn't a reluctant member of this courtship anymore, but that didn't mean his primary motive wasn't a sense of obligation to restore her reputation. She wanted him to like her, and despite what Christiana believed, she wasn't sure that he did.

Dr. Fiske's home was attractive as he was a man of some means. But one could tell he took care outfitting the dining room for great comfort, which made sense given he enjoyed eating so immensely. It was a wonder he stayed so slim. Abigail found the blue and cream walls restful. The large oval table made it easier to engage in group discussions. Instead of paintings, Dr. Fiske had beautiful versions of maps, star charts, and other interesting artifacts and conversation pieces, which he regularly changed. As much as Abigail loved researching with Dr. Fiske and Lord Darton, she also loved spending time with them in a non-research setting.

Abigail took a sip of her soup. "Dr. Fiske, this is delicious. What kind of soup is it? I'm not sure I've tasted anything quite like it."

"My cook calls it lobster bisque," Dr. Fiske replied. "He doesn't make it often, and it'll be harder now that winter is over."

Abigail gobbled it down. *I would have been happy just having that for dinner.* She enjoyed the beef, asparagus, and salad as well.

"Where'd you get the beef, Dr. Fiske?" asked Walter. "It's excellent."

"That's Crauford beef." Dr. Fiske replied. "Well worth the trip and the money. You won't get meat like this in a market."

Abigail tucked that in her memory banks. She wouldn't mind having this beef on their table either. A wave of contentment overtook Abigail, and she smiled at Lord Darton.

He stilled for a moment and then grinned back at her.

He's never smiled at me so affectionately before. And he must have purchased that vest in London because Abigail had never seen it before. It was a gold paisley color that made his blond hair seem more golden, and paired with the blue dinner coat that matched his eyes, Lord Darton looked quite striking. Her heart beat harder as she stuck another forkful of food in her mouth.

Then came the parade of desserts— pudding of all

kinds, iced orange, and pound cake. Abigail laughed. "Dr. Fiske, you've made enough for an army."

He smiled. "I just want everyone to enjoy themselves. Help yourself."

And help herself she did. She didn't bother with worrying about whether the quantities were proper or ladylike. She sampled everything like Dr. Fiske urged her and quite stuffed herself.

After a little more conversation, the three headed to their workspace in the attic. There was a lovely display of flowers, a box of chocolates, a mathematics book, and a fabulous looking spyglass by the windows.

"What's all this?" she exclaimed.

Lord Darton's eyes shone. "You like it?"

"Is this all for me?" she asked.

He bobbed his head up and down.

Abigail's jaw dropped. She was speechless as she slowly walked to the presents, picked up the spyglass, and looked through it. "This is lovely. I can see much further, and it's clearer. Thank you so much, Lord Darton. What's the occasion?"

He looked a little sheepish. "None. Just because. I'm very happy to be here. To see you." He paused. "And Dr. Fiske."

Dr. Fiske chuckled.

Before she knew what she was doing, Abigail threw her arms around Lord Darton's neck and gave him a tight hug. "I'm happy to see you too," she whispered.

Lord Darton held her for a moment, and Abigail reveled in his closeness and warmth. *This is wonderful. I could stay here just like this.* Then Dr. Fiske quietly suggested they get started, and the trio commenced work.

"It's back," Lord Darton said a couple of hours later.

Abigail looked up sharply from her desk as Dr. Fiske rushed towards the window.

"What is?" she asked.

"The comet," he said, his eye glued to the telescope. "It's much sooner than I expected."

Abigail joined them at the scope as Lord Walter started calling out information. Abigail and Dr. Fiske wrote it down furiously.

The numbers tumbled in Abigail's head. Shapes, calculations, equations, dates. She rushed back to the desk and began scribbling again.

"Abigail, I need you here—" Lord Darton started.

"I have to write this down before I lose it—"

"Lose what?" Lord Darton asked.

"Shapes. Orbits," Abigail replied. "It's in my head. I have to get it down before it's gone."

Two hours later, Abigail put her pen down. "Four years, three months. Two days." She turned. "Lord Darton, what was the exact date of when you first made the sighting?"

He rifled through papers on his desk and finally lifted one. "August 1st, 180_."

Then he gazed at Abigail like she was a wonderful creature. Her gaze locked with his intense blue one.

Dr. Fiske cleared his throat.

Abigail jumped in her seat.

"Congratulations." Dr. Fiske grinned. "I think you two have a paper to write."

Abigail and Lord Darton beamed at one another. *How marvelous to work with him on something as wonderful as this.* "You've been working with Dr. Fiske for over four years?" she asked him.

He nodded. "Closer to five."

"That's about the same time you began tutoring me," Abigail commented to Dr. Fiske.

"You finished your regular mathematics lessons at fifteen?" Lord Darton exclaimed.

Abigail's face grew hot again, and she looked away. "You can see why Mama wasn't pleased." She made a face. "She would've rather me attend a finishing school. Papa said if he brought in science and math tutors, he'd allow her to bring in anyone she wanted to mirror a proper finishing school education." Abigail exhaled, drawing a circle on the desk with her finger. "Enter the elocutionist," she muttered.

A mischievous smile played on Lord Darton's lips. "Well, Lady Abigail, you have wonderful inflection and superior voice modulation."

Abigail lifted her chin high. "Why thank you, Lord Darton," she said in the stuffiest, most mannerly drawl she could muster. "You should hear me at home in the privacy of my quarters as my voice can be dreadfully appalling," she finished, drawing out her vowels and l's.

Dr. Fiske smiled, shaking his head as Lord Walter laughed hard, his blue eyes twinkling and blond hair glistening in the candlelight.

Abigail watched him, her smile fading. *This is what we could have had.* A pang hit her. *When he first broke our engagement, my only real care was what it did to my reputation and not that we weren't together. That was of little value to me.* She sighed. *But I'm missing out on something wonderful and special because I'm not married to Lord Darton. The wedding would have been in just two weeks.*

"Lady Abigail, are you unwell?" Lord Darton asked quietly.

She shook her head. "I just had a thought..." She plastered on a smile. "It's nothing."

"It's something, Lady Abigail," he said gently, his eyes softening. "Please tell us if the telling will ease."

Her breath caught. *Where was this warm and kind man during their courtship?* He had been gentleman like and polite, but this was different. This was a Lord Darton she never knew existed.

She glanced at her hands in her lap. "I just realized how much I lost."

******

Walter

Walter's breathing got shallow as he gazed at Lady Abigail in the chair at her desk, her face flushed and gray eyes bright. *Is she afraid she's lost me? How can she not know how much I like her? I thought it was obvious. Even Dr. Fiske figured it out.*

"Lost what, Lady Abigail?" he asked, leaning forward.

Lady Abigail's cheeks reddened as she stared at the floor. "We could have been doing this all the time."

"Then it's good we got another chance," Walter said.

She nodded, still not meeting his eyes.

"Lady Abigail, please look at me," he said gently.

Abigail looked up, her eyes large and cheeks bright red.

"You haven't lost me," Walter said. "I'm more yours now than I ever was."

Lady Abigail flushed and looked down at her hands again.

"Our courtship is real to me," Walter said. "Not a scheme or a good business arrangement. And not just because we're well matched."

Lady Abigail beamed at him. "We are well matched. Just in ways neither one of us ever dreamed."

Walter took her hand and squeezed it gently. "Yes. Absolutely." *She has no idea. She's perfect for me.* "Then we're both in earnest now?"

Lady Abigail nodded vigorously, eyes shining.

"Excellent! I'll let Thurston know he's off the hook." Walter's grin turned more wry. "Or considering how willing he was to court you himself, maybe not welcome would be more accurate."

Lady Abigail gave a soft laugh, pressing a hand to her stomach. She looked fine tonight in a white dress which looked to be constructed of the lightest, flowing cloth, and she had another beautiful shawl of a deep red-violet print with gold trim.

This gorgeous woman is mine again, in truth now. Walter kissed her hand that was still in his and then scanned the room. "Where did Dr. Fiske get to?"

Lady Abigail looked about her. "I have no idea. I didn't even realize he was gone."

"Perhaps we find him and let him know he's off the hook too," he said.

Lady Abigail giggled as he pulled her from the chair and close to him. She took his arm, and the two slowly made their way down the stairs out of the attic.

CHAPTER 11

Mr. Yeatman

Abigail

Dr. Fiske invited Abigail and Walter for brunch and research three days later on Saturday since everyone had evening plans. All three were excited to work on the article, and Dr. Fiske had already submitted a brief announcement to the newspaper about Lord Darton's comet sighting. Abigail glanced at Lord Darton sitting next to her as she took a sip of water. *I can't believe we're courting in earnest again. I thought I'd lost him just when I realized how wonderful he was.*

The two of them couldn't stop grinning at one another.

Dr. Fiske groaned. "You two will make me sick if you keep doing that. Is this what it'll be like now?"

Lord Darton chuckled. "I'm sorry, Dr. Fiske, I'll try to control myself. Try being the operative word. I don't know if I can help it."

Dr. Fiske rolled his eyes. "Just finish up, so we can get to work, and you two can stop mooning over each other." He shook his head but then smiled.

If we publish this paper, it could be the beginning of a mathematics career for me. I never thought that possible, and I'll have accomplished it with a man I could marry who's smart and handsome and likes that I love math. It's perfect.

The door sounded, and a minute later, a servant showed a good-looking man with dark brown hair and deep blue eyes into the breakfast room. He stood before them, turning his hat in circles.

"Mr. Locke," Abigail whispered.

The man whipped his head towards her. "Yes, I'm Edgar Locke, and I deeply apologize for this intrusion. Miss Christiana Yeatman requested that I meet her here."

Dr. Fiske rose from his chair. "Christiana has yet to grace us with her presence," he said wryly. "People will begin to mistake my house for one of the assembly rooms."

Lord Darton chuckled.

"Dr. Fiske." He extended his hand towards Mr. Locke.

Mr. Locke shook it. "Again, I'm very sorry for intruding in your home in this manner and interrupting your meal. I had hoped Miss Yeatman would arrive first and make this less awkward."

"Take a seat," Dr. Fiske said. "Have you eaten?"

"I have. Thank you, sir." Mr. Locke sat in a chair, his back ramrod straight.

Abigail tried to give him a welcoming smile, and he returned it with a hesitant but friendly one. *I can see why Christiana likes him so. Despite his discomfort, he has a rather winning way to him.*

Dr. Fiske chuckled. "Relax. We're not sending you to the tower." He introduced Lord Walter and Abigail and then returned to his seat.

"Miss Christiana has spoken much of you," Mr. Locke said to Abigail. "She loves you like a sister."

"I feel the same affection for her, and I hope to become well acquainted with you," said Abigail.

"Do you like astronomy, Mr. Locke?" Dr. Fiske asked.

"I enjoy looking at the stars as much as anyone, sir," he replied. "But I can't say I have a full-fledged interest in astronomy."

"I like you," Dr. Fiske said. "You're precise. We'll keep you."

Christiana burst into the room.

"Ah, finally," Dr. Fiske said dryly, popping a cherry in his mouth.

Mr. Locke smiles upon Christiana as though she were a goddess. At least the affection runs deep both ways.

"What plot do you have afoot, Miss Christiana?" asked Dr. Fiske. "Every time one of you comes over now, it's like having a production of the Globe in my home."

Christiana plopped in a chair and grabbed a puffed pastry. "And we all know you love every minute of it, Dr. Fiske," she said with an airy wave of her hand. She then popped a piece of pastry in her mouth and closed her eyes.

Mr. Locke's eyes widened as he looked between Dr. Fiske and Christiana.

"We're a bit informal around here," said Lord Darton.

"These are fabulous," Christiana said. "I've never tasted anything like it." She opened her eyes. "I'd like to introduce everyone to Mr. Edgar Locke. We're courting."

Dr. Fiske snorted. "Yes, that's been covered adequately in your absence. What hasn't been explained is why you'd send this poor man to the home of another man whom he's never met to meet you."

"I need to borrow Abigail and Lord Darton," Christiana said.

"It's amazing how one explanation makes the situation even murkier," Dr. Fiske said.

Mr. Locke cracked a smile.

Lord Darton raised an eyebrow. "Borrow?"

"I claimed them first," said Dr. Fiske.

"You always have them." Christiana made a face towards Dr. Fiske. "You have to share."

"You're officially courting now?" Abigail asked her. "You spoke to your father?"

"That would be a no," replied Christiana. "Which is why I need you and Lord Darton. If Father sees the two of you, he may stand down. It'll be like vouching for Edgar—"

"I didn't think Mr. Locke's character was the issue," Lord Darton interrupted. "And I don't know him." He glanced at Mr. Locke. "No offense intended."

Mr. Locke shook his head. "None taken whatsoever. Your reasoning is sound."

"The person you need is Thurston," Lord Darton said.

Mr. Locke winced. "That won't happen."

"Is he displeased with you for some reason?" Lord Darton asked sharply.

"Lord Thurston wouldn't involve himself in this kind of personal matter," Mr. Locke replied. "He's a fair boss, we've known one another since childhood, and I dare say I probably enjoy a closer relationship with him than most others in the same situation. But he's still very much master."

Lord Darton nodded, sitting back in his chair. "It's a wonder you came to me then, Miss Christiana."

She waved a hand. "You're not like that. I mean, for a minute, when you messed up with Abigail, I thought you were. But you ate your hat and asked to court her again, so you're good people."

Lord Darton looked towards Abigail.

Outwardly supporting Christiana and Mr. Locke's court-ship could expose us to some comments and put us in a difficult situation. But if Christiana understands and accepts responsibility for the consequences of her actions, I have no issues with her courting and marrying Mr. Locke. She nodded at Lord Darton.

He gave Dr. Fiske a wan smile. "Would you mind if we—"

Dr. Fiske waved his hand. "No. Go. This is more important. But you two owe me."

"I don't know what practical good we'll do, but we'll come," Lord Darton said to Christiana.

"If you two are there, I'll feel like I have at least a little support," said Christiana.

Lord Darton smirked at her. "How do you know I support this?"

"I don't," admitted Christiana. "But I think you trust Abigail. You erred once before not trusting her, so I think you'll be careful not to do it again."

Lord Darton gazed towards Abigail, a slow smile lighting his face. "No. I won't do that again."

Abigail's heart thumped faster as she held his look.

✳✳✳✳✳✳

Walter

Miss Christiana had said her father was spending the next two weeks in the country, which was another reason why they needed chaperones to see him. It was a little over an hour's drive with plenty of woods, farms, and the occasional village to look at. Since the day was partially cloudy and he was unsure which way it would go, Walter preferred taking his carriage instead of one of his open conveyances.

Walter had played a little hard at Dr. Fiske's house, but Garret had spoken enough of Mr. Locke so that Walter's impression that he was a good man seemed to be a sound one. Garret credited much of the smooth operation of his largest mill to him. The workers liked Mr. Locke a great deal, and he acted as a good mediator between them and Garret. He had the reputation of being a diligent employee, very intelligent, and affable. It seemed in terms of merit, Miss Christiana chose well.

As foreman, Mr. Locke did very well financially for one of his station. But it was nothing like what Miss Christiana Yeatman was used to. The Yeatman's wealth exceeded Walter's, as it exceeded most noblemen. It comprised of a powerful combination of successful trade in shipping and a vast amount of property, which had slowly but steadily been increased over a couple of centuries. *I wonder how Christiana will make that massive adjustment.*

Mr. Locke courting Christiana was acting outside his station, and Walter would be expected to frown on that in his own circles. *I don't really disapprove. My only questions were of a practical nature.* He exhaled. *We'll have to see how this falls out.*

Mr. Locke had been quiet during the trip. *He must be in love with Miss Christiana to be willing to go up against her father. At least he's attempting to do things right. They could have just run off together.*

The mansion proper finally came into view. Walter had been here before but only in the evening for dinner parties and balls. This was the first time he viewed the estate in broad daylight, and it made a difference. Mr. Yeatman was a man of distinctive presence, and his country mansion complimented that personality. The home had three different sections, with the center one exhibiting a grand porch with four tall, thick columns and staircases on both sides. The property had a unique temple-like building in the distance, which Walter was pretty sure was for just show. It was attractive sitting on the hilltop and nestled within trees.

"You live here?" Mr. Locke asked Miss Christiana quietly.

She grinned. "Yes, this is home."

Mr. Locke exhaled.

The carriage reached the front door, and the four hopped out. The entranceway was a vast room itself, with not just one but two grand staircases on either side of the space, echoing the porch. Walter looked up towards the second floor where a huge painting of probably some ancestor or the other hung on the wall as though guarding the home.

Christiana informed the butler she'd like an audience with her father as soon as possible, and they would wait in the Italian room.

Mr. Locke looked about him, his eyes wide and mouth slightly ajar as they headed there. "I knew, but I had no idea, Christiana."

She plopped on a couch and patted the seat next to her. "Come and sit, Edgar dear." She grinned. "I'm still the same Christiana."

Lady Abigail sat in a chair facing them. Walter strolled around the room, taking in his surroundings. He assumed the Italian room was so named because of the decor and objects contained therein being Italian like in nature, though Walter didn't really have any idea of such things. The red walls and subjects of the paintings and sculptures lent the space a dramatic atmosphere. He recognized a Titian and wondered how the Yeatmans managed to procure it. Same with a sculpture on a marble pedestal that almost looked like a Bernini. Walter shook his head in wonder as he stared at the swirling, twisting figures that seemed to be fighting to get away from something.

The door opened about fifteen minutes later, and Christiana's father, Mr. Arnold Yeatman, made his entrance. He was a great big bear of a man. Christiana's features, though not her stature, were much like his. He had brown wavy hair that had not gone gray despite his age and light brown eyes.

Everyone jumped up.

"Father!" Christiana exclaimed. "We didn't expect you to come here. I thought we'd speak with you in the library."

"I'm sure you did," Mr. Yeatman said dryly. "Lord Darton and Lady Abigail, it's a pleasure to have you in my home." He cut Miss Christiana a look. "In the future, I hope we'll be given more notice so you can be received properly."

"Not at all, Mr. Yeatman," said Walter. "It's we who are intruding, and we've been entertained very well."

"Excellent. What can I do for you, Lord Darton?" Mr. Yeatman asked.

Walter paused a moment and glanced at Miss Christiana. Her face was flushed, and eyes flashing, while Mr. Locke's expression was blank.

This wasn't the position Walter expected to be in. It appeared Mr. Yeatman wanted to deal primarily with him. As a nobleman, Walter could understand that on a certain level. But Miss Christiana was Mr. Yeatman's daughter, and Walter had expected him to show her more attention than he had thus far.

"Lady Abigail and I accompanied Miss Yeatman and Mr. Locke as they have an important matter they wish to discuss with you," Walter explained.

"I don't doubt it," Mr. Yeatman crossed his arms. "What do you think of this important matter, Lord Darton?"

Walter studied him for a moment. *What game are we playing here, sir?* "I believe I need a more specific question, Mr. Yeatman. I agree the matter is important, and I wish for their happiness and well-being."

"You wish them success in this errand?" Mr. Yeatman asked.

Walter raised an eyebrow. "I believe this visit is more of an informative nature as opposed to obtaining any-thing."

Mr. Yeatman nodded and then stood in front of Miss Christiana and Mr. Locke, staring at them a moment.

"Father, we want—" Miss Christiana started.

Mr. Yeatman put a hand up, staring hard at Mr. Locke.

Mr. Locke, to his credit, held his gaze. *He has some backbone. More than one nobleman has withered under Mr. Yeatman's stare.*

"What is your business here, Mr. Locke?" asked Mr. Yeatman.

"Miss Yeatman and I are here to respectfully inform you of our courtship," Mr. Locke replied.

"And if I do not approve?" Mr. Yeatman asked.

"That will sadden us," replied Mr. Locke. "As we wish for good relations with you and Mrs. Yeatman. You also wield a great deal of influence, and your approval would sway the minds of many in Miss Yeatman's society." He paused. "But it'll not necessarily affect the status of our courtship."

Walter stifled a whistle.

"You answered well," said Mr. Yeatman. "Which makes what I'll have to do to you unfortunate." Mr. Yeat-man looked towards Miss Christiana. "You've acted fool-ishly, Christiana. You know you can't marry a foreman."

She squared her shoulders and raised her chin. "Watch me, Father."

"You believe you're ready?" Mr. Yeatman laughed loud and hard. "You have no idea, do you?" he asked with derision.

Walter exhaled. He didn't care for the way Mr. Yeatman was treating his daughter, but Walter suspected he spoke the truth. He exchanged a glance with Lady Abigail.

Christiana crossed her arms. "Don't think you can intimidate me—"

"It'll be more than intimidation," he snapped. "Do what you two like, but know I'll see to it that Mr. Locke is fired."

"Father!" Christiana exclaimed.

Mr. Locke set his jaw. "You're the type of man that would treat me in such a way?"

"I am," Mr. Yeatman replied. "And you're courting a woman who knowingly put you in that position. Be careful of your choice for wife."

Walter winced.

"I have nothing against your person, Mr. Locke." Mr. Yeatman directed a stern gaze towards Christiana. "But Christiana should perform her duty to her family and marry in or above her station. I feel that's a relatively simple demand, and I don't make many of her."

"It's an extraordinary thing to direct whom I should marry—" Christiana started.

"You have half the noblemen in the country at your doorstep," Mr. Yeatman said. "None of them suit you?"

"Nobility can be earned and granted, Mr. Yeatman," said Mr. Locke.

"You think you can make that happen, Mr. Locke?" Mr. Yeatman asked in an acerbic tone.

"I'm foreman of one of the richest textile mills in the country," Mr. Locke replied. "That was not by accident. I make things happen."

The room was silent for a moment.

"I won't direct who you marry, Christiana," said her father. "But disoblige me on this matter, and you better believe I'll put you through the fire to get what you want."

Miss Christiana and Mr. Yeatman engaged in a stare-down.

"I think our business is concluded, Mr. Locke," said Mr. Yeatman.

"I concur," Mr. Locke replied in a hard voice and eyes to match

Mr. Yeatman smirked at his daughter. "Enjoy your courtship."

Miss Christiana balled her fist and gritted her teeth while her father headed towards the door.

"Lord Darton and Lady Abigail, you're always most welcome here," Mr. Yeatman said. "And I wish you two a happy and successful courtship."

Lady Abigail winced as she curtsied.

"Thank you, Mr. Yeatman," Walter said evenly, and Mr. Yeatman exited the room.

"Argh!" Miss Christiana yelled.

Mr. Locke took her balled up fists in both his hands and pulled her into him. Her shoulders relaxed as she leaned her forehead against his for a moment. Mr. Locke tenderly kissed her head and took a step back.

Christiana exhaled and walked towards Lady Abigail and Walter. "I'm sorry. I had no idea he'd do that in front of the two of you." She grabbed his hands. "I'll never forget your words and actions here today and what you've done for Edgar and me. You have my deepest gratitude and utmost respect."

Walter bowed his head at her, touched. *I didn't do much, but I'm happy she's so pleased with it.* While Walter understood Mr. Yeatman's reservations, he acted in a most high-handed manner and spoke to Miss Christiana in a way to intentionally cause extreme embarrassment. *That's not appropriate, especially in the company of others.*

"Those were bold words there, Mr. Locke," said

Walter.

Mr. Locke rubbed his mouth. "Yes, I'm not sure what got into me there. Not that it's untrue..." he trailed off.

Walter chuckled.

"Christiana, do you wish to visit with anyone else while we're here?" Mr. Locke asked.

"No," she replied. "And I'm sure you'd like to leave this place."

"I'd rather not run into your father again," Mr. Locke said dryly.

Miss Christiana chuckled. "Then let's depart. We've accomplished our goal. Father knows, and you'll be courting me openly."

Mr. Locke held his arm out, and Miss Christiana took it.

"Which is what I wanted," he said. "No more hiding,"

Christiana nodded. "No more hiding."

******

They'd been driving for a little while when Miss Christiana suggested they stop for a bit and enjoy a pretty piece of countryside. She grabbed Mr. Locke's hand after they got out of the carriage and gave Lady Abigail a jaunty wave. "We'll see you in a little bit."

Lady Abigail raised an eyebrow. "A very little bit."

Miss Christiana laughed, and the two of them headed off towards a nearby stream.

I don't mind at all. Walter threaded his fingers through Abigail's and winked at her. "Let's see what's in the opposite direction."

Lady Abigail reddened but nodded, and the two took off.

After a short time, she released Walter's hand and put her arm through his. "What you did with Mr. Yeatman was very good." She smiled at him. "I was very impressed."

Walter's chest swelled. They sat in a grassy area under a willow tree by another brook. Abigail still had her arm tucked in his and laid her head on his shoulder.

"I'd like to kiss you, Abigail," Walter said quietly.

She chuckled. "You've done it before, Walter, and never asked. We were engaged once."

"I just wanted to make sure I didn't scandalize your proper lady senses by kissing you relatively early in our second courtship."

Lady Abigail threw her head back and laughed.

"You never laughed like that when we were together before," Walter said.

"You were never so clever and entertaining before." She sobered. "I feel like I'm myself with you now."

"Me too." Walter leaned down and gave Abigail a gentle kiss. *This is nothing like the ones we had before.* He kissed her again more firmly. *It's like I belong to her.*

She flushed. "You never kissed like that when we were together before."

Walter barked out a laugh. "Was I that disappointing?"

"Disappointing isn't quite the word I'd use. It was nice."

He snorted. "Nice?"

Lady Abigail shrugged. "You know, a pleasant experience."

Walter chuckled. "You certainly know how to destroy a man's pride. So, what was that?"

She grinned mischievously. "That was not nice, and I liked it a lot."

Walter smiled back. "Then let's do one more, shall we?"

Lady Abigail was still giggling as Walter leaned in and kissed her once again.

CHAPTER 12

Gossip Wheel

Abigail

Elise Wyndham, the Baroness of Broughton, had put together a project for the noblewomen in the Bath area to create needlepoint pieces that could be sold in select shops, and the proceeds would go to the local orphanage. Periodically, she hosted needlepoint parties, where the women could work on their pieces together. Since the Wyndhams were in Bath presently, this party was at a home they rented in town instead of at their estate.

While Abigail liked the project itself and enjoyed Lady Broughton's company, she didn't care for the connected parties. They were always rife with gossip, and since she'd been the object of such careless talk, it was even more objectionable to her than it had been before.

But Mama had said it'd be a good idea for her to attend. Abigail's surprise renewed courtship with Lord Darton had set the most vicious tongues in place, but Mama pointed out she could further silence matters by taking her place among everyone. Abigail didn't like the idea but had to admit Mama's advice was sound.

"The St. Clare women!" Lady Broughton's brown eyes danced as she greeted them in the entranceway. "Now I know I'm in posh society."

"Lady Broughton, you're too kind," Lady Belden said. "Thank you for the invitation."

"I'm so happy you're here." Lady Broughton looked towards Abigail. "May I ask a favor of you?"

Abigail raised an eyebrow. "Certainly."

"My fourteen-year-old daughter has been dying to meet you, especially since she heard you were coming here," Lady Broughton said. "She believes you're the most ladylike of young ladies. Do you mind being introduced to her?"

"I'm honored to have such a compliment paid to me, though I'm sure I don't deserve it," Abigail replied. "I'd be delighted."

Lady Broughton smiled at her. "There it is, the most ladylike of ladies. The butler will take your things, and my daughter will be down in just a second."

Less than a minute later, a pretty girl with light brown, curly hair, beautiful green eyes, and a smattering of freckles across her nose raced down the stairs. She grinned, and Abigail smiled back.

"Lady Abigail, I'd like to present my daughter Portia," said Lady Broughton. "Portia, this is Lady Abigail St. Clare."

Portia curtsied. "I'm so happy to make your acquaintance. Your outfit is to die for."

She has good taste. It was a Parisian outfit that Abigail loved, but a few others had thought it was very modern looking. She didn't mind that, but apparently looking modern was one of the seven deadly sins to some. The dress had a delicate fringe at the bodice, and the pink coat with the fur edging and the matching bonnet was, as Portia said, to die for. It would probably be the last time Abigail could wear it for a while as it was getting too warm.

Lady Broughton shook her head. "Portia, dear."

"I can't wait until I'm out in society," Portia continued. "And I hope to court a man as handsome as Lord Darton. He is such a fine man."

"Portia!" Lady Broughton exclaimed.

Abigail leaned towards Portia. "I agree with you whole-heartedly." Abigail winked at her, and the girls giggled.

"Portia, let the ladies go to the party," said her mother.

I think I might enjoy myself more with Portia.

"It was lovely meeting you," Portia said.

"I'm glad to have met you too," Abigail replied. "I'm sure we'll see one another again."

Lady Broughton linked arms with Abigail as they headed out of the entranceway. "Thank you so much. You've probably made her month."

Abigail smiled. "Again, I don't think I deserve such high praise, but I'm happy if Portia is so pleased. She seems like a lively girl, and she's very pretty."

"Yes, and lively she is." Lady Broughton laughed.

The women entered the drawing room, and the St. Clares were announced.

Abigail surveyed the group. Lady Broughton had a decent showing today. *Lady Darton is here as well. Perhaps I can spend some time with her.*

Lady Abigail made her way to where Lady Darton was seated with several other women. She said hello to everyone and sat down.

All the ladies smiled and greeted her back, except Lady Darton. She only nodded in her direction— without a smile.

Abigail joined the conversation.

Lady Darton didn't look at her or acknowledge her.

Abigail shifted in her chair. *Surely Lord Darton has discussed what transpired. She can't still be so upset with me, can she?*

After engaging in further chit chat with the other ladies in which Lady Darton didn't participate, Abigail turned her attention squarely on her. "Lord Darton told me you enjoyed looking at the stars."

Lady Darton didn't take her eyes off her needlepoint. "He is correct."

Abigail swallowed. *She's making this very difficult.* "I enjoy it as well. Perhaps one evening we could do so together."

"If you insist upon it," Lady Darton said coldly.

Abigail stared at her a moment. "I don't insist at all. I just thought it would be pleasant—"

Lady Darton sighed and stood. "If you will excuse me, I require a drink of water."

Abigail's jaw dropped as she stared after Lady Darton walking away.

One of the other ladies raised an eyebrow. "Well, that was just a touch rude if you ask me, though Lady Darton never won any contests for being warm and fuzzy, if you know what I mean."

A couple of the other ladies chuckled.

Abigail forced a smile. "Perhaps she's unwell today."

Another lady smirked. "She must be unwell a lot."

They all tittered.

Abigail sighed. *This is exactly why I don't enjoy these gatherings in the first place.* Granted, she didn't care for Lady Darton's manner either, but she didn't want it to be fodder amongst the needlepoint group. She caught sight of one of the lady's screens. "That's a unique design. Did you create it yourself?"

The lady began an enthusiastic explanation of how she developed the idea.

Lady Abigail tried to be attentive, but her mind wandered. *Lady Darton really doesn't like me. Is it my work with Dr. Fiske that has her so upset with me now? Or maybe Lord Darton never explained?*

Abigail frowned. *Lord Darton is not like Christiana. Heavy opposition from his mother may lead him to end our courtship. Again.*

"Anything the matter, Lady Abigail?" one of the ladies asked.

Abigail forced another smile. "Something I can attend to later. I apologize for not being better company."

Lady Edith took the seat Lady Darton had just left.

Abigail barely suppressed a groan.

"Lady Darton sure left this spot in a huff." Lady Edith smirked. "You seem to have a natural flair for upsetting her a great deal."

Abigail gritted her teeth. "Do you require something of me, Lady Edith?"

"I just thought I'd offer my assistance." She lowered her voice and whispered, "Sometimes it's hard to negotiate the old guard."

"It's not a fencing match," retorted Abigail.

"Is it not? I think the duels we're playing here are just as deadly." She arched an eyebrow. "Wouldn't you agree?"

Abigail swallowed. It's not often she agreed with Lady Edith, but on that point, she hit the proverbial nail on its head.

"I think I may have a little more finesse. Though I must say, you finessed your way back to Lord Darton. But I suspect you won't keep him if you don't find a way to his mother." Lady Edith smirked. "I'm willing to offer guidance anytime. She's even sought my company on a few occasions."

Abigail pressed her lips together. *Something she has never done with me.*

Lady Edith rose. "As a matter of fact, I'll see to her now."

It was all Abigail could do to keep from growling at her retreating back.

✶✶✶✶✶✶

Walter

"Mr. Locke!" Walter exclaimed. "I'm surprised to see you here." They were on the pavements outside of Garret's home in Bath. It was a pleasant surprise, as Walter liked Mr. Locke more and more every time he was in his company. In the two weeks since the trip to Miss Christiana's country home, they'd all been in company together several times.

Walter extended his hand, and Mr. Locke pumped it. "Good morning, Lord Darton. I frequently meet with Lord Thurston here instead of him coming to the mill."

It was a windy day, and Walter put a hand on his hat to steady it. "I hear there may be some exciting changes coming."

"Yes. We had a demonstration a couple of days ago for the new loom," said Mr. Locke.

"So soon? And what's the verdict?"

"It's very impressive," replied Mr. Locke. "We were just discussing how we could best incorporate it into our production. The machines are expensive and large, and the punch card setup will require some know-how."

Walter grinned. "Were you nominated to learn the process?"

Mr. Locke chuckled. "I do seem to be the top candidate at the moment."

"How are things otherwise?" Walter asked.

Mr. Locke sobered. "They're good."

"Come, what's troubling you?"

"I don't want to keep you from your visit," replied Mr. Locke. "And this is perhaps not the best place to expound on things."

"Let's leave then. We can head to the Upper Rooms—"

Mr. Locke smiled. "Lord Darton, you're a good man. I believe you forget I'm a foreman. I really do need to return to work."

Walter chuckled. "You're right, of course." *Mr. Locke reads like a gentleman. I understand why Miss Christiana is pushing this relationship.* "I'll be at Dr. Fiske's tonight. If you'd like to come by after you're finished at the mill, you're most welcome. Lady Abigail won't be present as she has a prior engagement."

"Are you sure you wish me there?" Mr. Locke asked carefully.

Walter gave him what he hoped was an encouraging smile. "I do. I vouched for you, remember?"

Mr. Locke glanced towards the ground and then nodded his head. "I'll be there. Thank you, Lord Darton."

Walter stared after him a moment as he walked down the street. *He seems to be a cautious and conservative man by nature. Miss Christiana must have made him lose his senses for him to decide to carry on a relationship with her.*

******

"That's odd," Dr. Fiske muttered while he moved some items around on his desk later that day. "I seem to be missing a paper."

Walter chuckled. "It's a wonder you notice with the mess on your desk." Dr. Fiske's desks were the only areas in his life that Walter had ever witnessed unkempt.

Dr. Fiske gave him a look. "It looks like chaos, but I understand the order."

Walter laughed harder.

"Ah, here it is," said Dr. Fiske. "But I'm positive I didn't leave it there."

"Perhaps Lady Abigail referenced it and thought she was putting it away." Walter smirked.

Dr. Fiske gave him another look. "Perhaps."

"I told Mr. Locke to stop by so we could discuss something," Walter said.

"Is he taking an interest in astronomy?" Dr. Fiske grinned. "We could form a club."

"I didn't ask, but you're free to float the notion when he arrives." He sobered. "Something is troubling him, and I believe it's to do with Miss Christiana."

Dr. Fiske snorted. "I don't doubt it."

"Are you against the match?"

"I don't know either of them well enough to form a strong opinion," Dr. Fiske replied. "But their different stations will present real challenges even without Miss Christiana's father being Mr. Yeatman."

"Mr. Yeatman threatened to have Mr. Locke fired."

Dr. Fiske grimaced. "I can see him acting on that and succeeding."

"I tried to feel Thurston out a little earlier today as to whether he'd do it if pressured by Mr. Yeatman."

"You do well to be careful yourself, Harding. Mr. Yeatman will be more gracious with you since you're an earl, but he does have his limits. You don't want to be caught in the crossfire. I can't imagine an estate of your size doesn't have business dealings with a man that casts a shadow as long as Mr. Yeatman's."

"I know, but Miss Christiana is Lady Abigail's closest friend, and Lady Abigail was so distressed..." Walter trailed off.

Dr. Fiske chuckled. "Your heart is caught up in this as well. Do as you must; I'm just advising you exercise caution."

"Your advice is well taken, and I thank you for it."

A couple of hours later, Mr. Locke joined them in the attic. "This is quite the setup. Does Miss Yeatman join you often?"

Dr. Fiske snorted.

"Miss Christiana is a new addition," Walter jumped in. "While she may take a turn at the scope on occasion, I wouldn't describe her as an avid astronomer," he explained. "Pull up a chair and tell me what troubles you, Mr. Locke."

"I can't support Miss Yeatman without my position, Lord Darton," said Mr. Locke as he sat alongside him. "She'll live below her station and far below her current lifestyle even with my position. I justified things knowing that as a foreman at Lord Thurston's mill, I have a very respectable place, and while we won't be landed gentry, we could be very comfortable middling."

Walter nodded. "Of course."

"I can't give her multiple homes and carriages and such. But we can have a large and pleasant cottage, and I could keep several servants for her. But if I lose my position..." He trailed off and shook his head. "I would be hard-pressed to find another to match it."

Dr. Fiske drummed his fingers on his desk. "You could be a steward, Mr. Locke. And it would afford you the same kind of living you enjoy now."

"Wasn't your father a steward?" Walter asked. He thought Garret had mentioned such.

"He was," replied Mr. Locke. "And I trained in those responsibilities with the expectation of taking over. But then Lord Thurston's father asked me to become foreman instead, and so here we are. I'm glad for it because I find this work more enjoyable."

"Coming from Lord Thurston's estate and mill would carry a lot of weight," said Dr. Fiske.

"Not if Mr. Yeatman destroys my reputation," Mr. Locke grumbled.

Dr. Fiske sighed. "There is that."

"This might not be comforting, but I believe Mr. Yeatman was sincere when he said he had no personal qualms with you," Walter said.

"I'd find that hard to believe since I'm taking his only daughter from him." Mr. Locke played with the brim of his hat on his lap. "It'd be hard for him to not have a personal issue with me just for that. If he truly hasn't, then he has a peculiar way of showing it."

"He's a peculiar man and has a peculiar relationship with Miss Christiana," said Walter. "She's always been a little defiant, and her father is sometimes not the pleasantest of men. Their personalities will make a difficult situation even harder to navigate. That being said, I believe that while he may carry out his threat, he would do so in a way that would do the least damage to your name. His only issues are your station and Miss Christiana defying him."

Mr. Locke raised an eyebrow. "Those are huge issues, Lord Darton."

"They are," conceded Walter. "But Mr. Yeatman has an extraordinary ability to compartmentalize and organize, which is probably one of the reasons why his business endeavors are so successful. He's attacking your job because it's the one thing that could make you crumble. Based on his words, I dare say there's a part of him that respects you."

Mr. Locke sighed. "I always knew he was not a man to be crossed, and of course, I manage to cross him in the worst possible way. I didn't want things to happen like this."

Walter clapped his shoulder. "Don't lose heart. While it's good to plan and think of different contingencies, the event hasn't happened yet. There may still be a way to work this out more amicably." *Though I'm at a loss as to how at the moment.*

Mr. Locke nodded.

"Just keep in mind why you're doing this," Walter said.

Mr. Locke's face lit up. "Yes. Miss Yeatman is more than worth the battle."

CHAPTER 13

Second Fiddle

Abigail

Typically, Abigail and Lord Darton spent Mondays, Wednesdays, and Fridays at Dr. Fiske's house researching, and Lord Darton called on her separately another day of the week. During their first courtship, Lord Darton had called on Abigail only once a week, and they'd see one another at social events. To be honest, she'd been satisfied with that. Abigail saw him far more often now, and it still didn't feel like enough.

The day after the needlepoint party, Lord Darton called and asked if she'd like to go for a ride, and she happily accepted. As Abigail was putting on her bonnet and gloves, he asked what she did the day prior since she missed working with them, and she told him about the party.

"Mother also attended," he said. "She didn't mention seeing you there."

"I'm not astonished," Abigail commented.

He stared at her. "Did you not have opportunity to be in each other's company?"

"No, we spoke with one another."

"I don't understand."

Abigail sighed. "Lord Darton, I'm afraid your mother has never warmed to me."

It's more than that, but she is his mother, so I'll be gentle. She finished tying her bonnet and started for the door. "It's not important now. Let's depart for our ride."

"I told you before she's always been reserved." Lord Darton said behind her. "She's not like Miss Christiana."

Abigail gave him a look. "I'm aware of that, but there's a difference between reserve and coolness."

He narrowed his eyes. "Mother is not a cold person."

"She doesn't like me. And she doesn't disguise the fact."

"She doesn't know you well," he said, his voice tighter.

"Then why have my attempts to correct that situation been cut short by her?" Abigail cried out. "It's as if she doesn't want to get to know me."

Lord Darton set his jaw. "With an attitude like that, it's no wonder. I wouldn't want to either."

Abigail's jaw dropped, and then she glared at him. "It's a wonder that you're taking the trouble now."

"You're quite right," Walter retorted. "I apologize, Lady Abigail, for I've just recalled a pressing errand I need to perform and must cancel our ride together."

Abigail crossed her arms. "And what would that be?"

"I need a haircut."

Abigail growled.

"At the moment, I'd rather be with the barber than you." Lord Darton smashed his hat onto his head. "Good day to you, Lady Abigail."

She gave him a curt nod, and he walked out of the house.

Abigail stood frozen for a moment and then pulled off her gloves. *That was our first real argument since we started courting again in earnest, and it's over something important.*

"I thought you and Lord Darton were to go on a ride?" Mama asked, walking into the entranceway.

Abigail found it hard to untie her bonnet. "He had an appointment he suddenly recalled and left."

Mama was quiet a moment. "Would you like to take some tea with me in my sitting room?"

"Yes, I would." Mama aggravated her many times, but there were moments when she seemed to know just what Abigail needed.

"Put your things away and come to me when you're ready."

Mama patted her arm, and Abigail followed her up the stairs. *Lady Darton has been the figure behind our most serious relationship woes. Why?*

******

Walter

Walter entered Dr. Fiske's study the next day tense. He'd considered not coming at all as he had no wish to see Lady Abigail. *Maybe if I work separately and don't engage her in conversation, I'll make it through the session.*

"It appears Lady Abigail won't be joining us this evening," Dr. Fiske said, looking towards a note on his desk.

Walter grunted. *Good. That solves my problem.* His headache faded.

Dr. Fiske raised an eyebrow at him. "Is all not right in lover's paradise?"

"It'd be fine if she weren't so discourteous towards my mother," Walter replied.

Dr. Fiske leaned back in his chair, studying Walter. "Lady Abigail is unconventional for sure, but I've never witnessed her being discourteous towards anyone, even as a girl of fifteen. What did she say? Perhaps this was just a misunderstanding."

Walter snorted. "I fully apprehended Lady Abigail's meaning. She essentially said my mother was a cold person who's resisted her attempts to draw closer to her. She even said Mother didn't want to get to know her."

"So, your mother has never brooked opposition towards your courtship with Lady Abigail?"

Walter was quiet a moment. "The only time was when she believed Lady Abigail was inconstant, which was understandable."

"Yes, but she also condemned her without having an audience with her." He paused. "Generally, that's not how a person acts towards one to whom they're disposed."

"We should get to work." Walter started towards the door of the study. *I should cease avoiding this just because I might not want to hear it.* "What are you attempting to say?"

Dr. Fiske sighed. "Lady Abigail will not put up with playing second fiddle to your mother."

Walter's body tensed. "I've never put her in that position."

Dr. Fiske gave him a look. "Come now, Harding. Be honest with yourself. When Lady Abigail's interests squarely oppose your mother's, your mother wins. I'm warning you that Lady Abigail will not put up with that indefinitely."

Walter stared out the window.

"I'm sorry. I didn't mean to upset you," Dr. Fiske said. "I understand the desire to be loyal to a parent, but you do well to at least entertain the thought that Lady Abigail's perceptions are true. You'll need to set that matter straight if you intend to make her your wife."

Walter set his jaw. "If Lady Abigail intends to be my wife, she needs to respect my mother."

"Certainly, and I'm sure she wants to do just that. But I believe she'll also look for her husband to offer support, and that's a reasonable expectation."

Silence filled the room.

Walter rubbed his forehead, still staring out the window. *I don't want Abigail to feel unprotected and without support. She's such a capable person; it's hard to believe she'd feel that way. And requiring protection from my mother is a situation that's hard to wrap my mind around.* "For one who's not married, you have a lot to say on the subject of courtship and marriage," Walter said.

Dr. Fiske chuckled. "Why do you think I never married, Harding? I could have, you know."

"Were you the victim of a tragic romance?" Walter asked.

Dr. Fiske laughed. "No, not at all. I courted a couple of ladies and decided married life wasn't for me. So I rented the country house out, gave my land agent more responsibilities and staff, and came here."

"Gave up the gentleman's life?"

Dr. Fiske shrugged. "That wasn't for me either. Being the second son, it's not like I got the family estate, which is why I did my medical studies. But when my uncle left me a sizable estate that he had received through a second cousin or some such, I decided to give it a try." He shook his head. "I'm much happier here. I can live a simpler existence, pursue the things I want, and still spend money on what's important to me."

Walter chuckled. "Like the lightest cherry filled pastries ever tasted?"

Dr. Fiske grinned. "Exactly."

I'm not Dr. Fiske though. I want the nobleman's life, and I want it with Lady Abigail. But that means I may have to make some hard decisions.

******

Abigail

The Monday following her argument with Lord Darton, Abigail took her frustrations out on the poor piano in the morning room, pounding on the keys when the butler announced Lord Darton was there to see her.

Lady Abigail stifled a sigh. *I guess I can't avoid him forever.* "Please take him to the drawing room, and I'll receive him there."

Abigail hadn't decided how she wanted to proceed. The thought of being put off by Lady Darton, and Lord Darton dismissing it as Abigail's fault, sent a chill through her. *That's not a life I want. All the astronomy and math in the world won't make up for that.* She didn't want to end the courtship, but at the same time forging on wasn't bringing her the same sense of contentment and happiness that it had before.

I'll see what Lord Darton has to say and go from there.

"Lady Abigail." He bowed low when Abigail entered the drawing room.

That's a good sign. Abigail curtsied. "Lord Darton."

"I must apologize for the way I left you the other day. It was most rude."

"My behavior didn't recommend itself either. I apologize as well."

Lord Darton gave her a wobbly smile.

Abigail returned it with a wan one.

They stood in silence for a moment, the only sound coming from a bird squawking outside the window.

"Are you working with us this afternoon?" Lord Darton asked.

Abigail hadn't been sure, but now that he had apologized, she'd rather research. Even if they hadn't addressed the core problem, his apology indicated he acknowledged there was one. She nodded. "I'll be there."

"Wonderful. My driver and I can escort you there and home if you wish to stay later into the evening."

Abigail's eyes widened. He'd done that before, but not regularly, as such a gesture depended on his schedule. "Thank you, I'd like that very much."

Lord Darton smiled. "Dr. Fiske and I will come later this afternoon to bring you there." He headed towards the door and then stopped short. "Lady Abigail, I want to assure you of my deepest admiration and respect."

Abigail looked at the floor, her face growing warm. "Thank you, Lord Darton."

They stood quietly for a moment.

"It's been brought to my attention that in my belief of your capableness, I haven't supported you the way I ought."

Abigail wrinkled her brow. "We've worked together for many weeks now. Things were perhaps rocky in the very beginning, but you've repeatedly commented on your confidence in my abilities."

"There's more to life than just science, Lady Abigail. I've been found wanting in those other areas. I'll endeavor to do better," Lord Darton said. "I'll return in a few hours."

Abigail stared at the door long after he had walked through it.

******

Walter

It was several hours after Walter had called on Lady Abigail, and the three of them were in the attic of Dr. Fiske's home as planned. He was happy he'd been able to cross that chasm with her, but they still hadn't addressed the core reason for their argument.

His mother.

At some point, that had to be discussed if their relationship was to move forward. *And I have every intention of having Lady Abigail as my wife. I'm just afraid I'm about to botch it up. Again.*

The day was warm, and Dr. Fiske had one of the windows open to let in a breeze that carried a faint fragrance.

"Hmm," Lady Abigail mumbled.

"May I be of assistance?" asked Lord Darton.

Lady Abigail bit her lip. "I'm missing a sheet of scratch paper."

"Why would you want that?" asked Dr. Fiske. "I usually discard mine."

"I do as well, in time," replied Lady Abigail. "But I prefer to keep all my work in case I need to review my findings or figure out a better way to explain the math to others."

Dr. Fiske nodded. "That's smart."

"It's not important," Lady Abigail said. "I can redo it. I just rather not if I don't have to."

Dr. Fiske's housekeeper appeared at the door, informing him of the arrival of someone.

Dr. Fiske's face lit up. "Excellent! I'll be down directly." He grinned at them. "I'm about to hire another cook."

Walter raised an eyebrow. "Another? Isn't one enough for just yourself?"

"Theoretically, yes," replied Dr. Fiske. "But this way, my French cook can concentrate on specialty foods and treats, while the other can be in charge of my more mundane day-to-day meals."

Lady Abigail smiled. "It sounds like a marvelous idea."

"I'm quite excited," Dr. Fiske said. "We'll really be eating well. You can tell Miss Christiana to take all the pastries she wants the next time she comes."

Lady Abigail threw her head back and laughed as Dr. Fiske left the room.

After a little while, Walter laid down the book he was consulting. *We need to talk, but I don't want to end up arguing. How do I broach this topic?*

Lady Abigail glanced at him. "Anything the matter?"

Walter cleared his throat. "Yes."

Lady Abigail raised an eyebrow and laid down her pen.

He leaned forward. "Do you truly feel my mother is cold towards you?"

She stared at him a moment. "I do."

She must be wrong. There's no way Mother would— He shook his head as he remembered Dr. Fiske's words about at least entertaining the thought that Abigail's perceptions were accurate on some level. "Would it ease your mind if I spoke to her about it?"

Lady Abigail's eyes widened. "Yes, it would. Thank you."

"I'm sure it's a misunderstanding, and once I bring it to her attention, things will be okay."

"I hope that's the case." She hesitated. "But if it's not?"

Walter swallowed. "I don't know." He paused. "The only thing I know for sure is that I'm not giving you up."

Lady Abigail's cheeks turned a light pink. "I don't want that either. But I can't...There are certain things I need..." she trailed off for a moment. Then she took a deep breath and squared her shoulders. "I don't want to be sacrificed every time your mother's will conflicts with my welfare and needs."

Walter nodded. "Of course. I promise you I'll make this right."

CHAPTER 14

Tea

Walter

"Mother, have you spent any time with Lady Abigail since we began courting?" Walter asked the next day after breakfast in the morning room.

Lady Darton was quiet a moment. "Of course."

Walter studied her. "In what capacity?"

"I see her on a regular basis at various functions, Walter."

"Do you speak with her at length?"

His mother rose from her chair and headed towards the sideboard. "Lady Abigail is quite popular," she said wryly. "I don't believe she speaks with anyone at length as she tends to circulate."

Walter narrowed his eyes. "She'd make an exception with you." He paused. "Have you sought her company outside of these functions? Called on her, for example? I know she's attempted to call on you a few times."

"Lady Abigail is very busy—"

"Have you tried, Mother?" he asked in a firm voice.

She stared at him. "No."

He exhaled. *This is not the position I wish to be in. I don't want to be forced to choose between my mother and Abigail. I love them both.* "Lady Abigail is under the distinct impression that you don't like her at all, and with this information, I can see why she'd form that belief."

"And what would you have me do about that?" his mother snapped. "Lady Abigail is a woman of her own mind. She's free to believe as she chooses and often does."

Walter gaped at her. *Lady Abigail was right.* "It'd be good if you were more welcoming, Mother. Lady Abigail almost became my wife before, and if things continue the way I wish, she'll become so this time. I'd like for the two most important women in my life to get along with one another. And the breakdown is with you, not Lady Abigail."

His mother stared towards the bay window and garden and then took a sip of water.

"Mother?" Walter prompted.

"Very well then, Walter." She set the glass down on the sideboard, her face blank and blue-gray eyes unreadable. "Would it suit you if I invited her to take tea with me this week?"

Walter smiled. "Yes, that would please me very much."

*****

"Miss Christiana!" Walter exclaimed as he entered Garret's drawing room early Wednesday afternoon. The room seemed to be an ode to oak, given the wall color and the furniture. He'd come to call on Garret before heading to Dr. Fiske's home and hadn't expected to find Miss Christiana there.

Miss Christiana gave him a strained smile. "Hello, Lord Darton. It's good to see a friend."

Walter's smile faded as he took a seat next to her. "What's happened?"

"Father carried out his threat," she replied. "I'm here to plead for Edgar's position."

Walter frowned. *It was expected, but now that the event has occurred...* He rubbed his face. "Has Thurston fired him?"

"No. Not yet," Miss Christiana replied. "But I fear it'll only be a matter of time."

Garret entered the room and grinned at them. "We'd be an unusual trio but entertaining. What scheme do you two have on hand?"

"I wish my visit were for pleasure, but I'm here on business," said Miss Christiana.

Lord Garret grew sober. "I wager you heard I had a visit from your father."

"There's no better man out there than Mr. Locke. Please keep him."

Garret stared at her a moment and then turned towards Walter. "And what was your errand here?"

"I did come to call," Walter replied. "I just learned of Mr. Yeatman's visit to you."

"It's an interesting situation," Garret said. "Though not surprising."

"I'll speak on behalf of Mr. Locke as well," Walter said. "I implore you not to fire him, though I realize that may be at great cost to yourself. I dislike the fact that Mr. Yeatman is using his influence in this manner."

"Mr. Locke shouldn't send you to beg for him," Garret said. "He knew his actions would have repercussions."

"He hasn't asked me to do any such thing," Walter said. "And he'd probably be uncomfortable with the fact that I am because he'd be aware of how it'd look."

"He needs his position," Miss Christiana said quietly, her eyes very large and round.

"You should have thought of those things before you began courting him," Garret retorted. "I had told you to leave him alone."

Miss Christiana cringed.

"You know your father," Garret went on. "Did you honestly believe you were going to do this without any recriminations towards Mr. Locke?" He put his hands on his hips. "You need to do better by him. There are fine women in his station who'd be a support instead of a hindrance to his success."

Miss Christiana paled. "Is that how you view me? As a hindrance? That I'm bad for him?"

Garret exhaled. "You're a fine woman, Miss Christiana, and I have told him so. But your differences in stations are more than just a snob thing. There are very real and practical considerations in terms of the different lives you two lead. Mr. Locke may not be gentry, but he's a fine man too and deserves a woman who can complement him. Bear that in mind."

Miss Christiana looked towards the floor.

"So, you're letting him go?" Walter asked.

"Of course not," Garret said firmly.

Miss Christiana jerked her head up and beamed at him.

"It'd be business suicide to let him go," Garret continued. "I'm embarking on one of the biggest changes my mills have seen in years, and Mr. Locke is learning and implementing the technology and changing the operations accordingly. No, Mr. Yeatman can go if he pleases." Garret smirked. "We'll figure out a way around him, and then he'll be back."

Walter raised an eyebrow. *This might be an interesting power play— the old guard versus the new.* Garret was one of the few people that Walter had seen willing to go toe-to-

toe with Mr. Yeatman. Besides Mr. Locke. *I guess they come from the same stock; no wonder they work well together.*

"This development, however, does necessitate the need for me to come up with some contingency plans, and read Mr. Locke the riot act." He gave Walter a wry smile. "Can we gallivant another day?"

Walter stood and grinned. "Of course, I completely understand. I can leave for Dr. Fiske's home a little early."

"Will Abigail be there?" Miss Christiana asked Walter.

"Most likely," he replied.

"May I accompany you?" she asked. "I don't want to be at my home with Father, and I could use some of Dr. Fiske's pastries or something while I whine at Abigail."

Garret rolled his eyes.

Walter chuckled. "Yes, you may come along."

******

Twenty minutes later, they were drying off in Dr. Fiske's parlor. The rain was unusually cool and damp for this time of year. Dr. Fiske had just started a good fire, and even though it was the end of May, it felt good.

Walter shook the rain off him. "I'm glad I took the carriage. I almost didn't."

A door slammed, and quick footsteps moved through the hallway.

Walter grinned. *Lady Abigail will be pleased with Mother's tea invitation. I can't wait to give it to her.*

Miss Christiana's eyes widened when Lady Abigail entered the room. "You're drenched!"

Lady Abigail twisted her face as she fought to pull her gloves off. "I feel disgusting, and I must look a sight."

She looks rather fine to me. Lady Abigail was flushed, and her gray eyes were bright. She removed her bonnet.

"Sit by the fire," Miss Christiana said, guiding Lady Abigail to a rug in front of the hearth. "You'll catch cold. And you should pull your hair down and dry it as well. It's a mess anyway."

Lady Abigail set to work, pulling down her hair.

Walter's jaw dropped. *She has the most amazing river of straight, rich brown hair.*

Lady Abigail glanced at him and blushed. "I should do this upstairs or just go home."

"No!" Walter exclaimed. "Please don't go."

Miss Christiana laughed. "He's helpless. Just stay, Abigail. You're already a little drier. Another hour and you should be fine."

"I might as well read something then," Lady Abigail said. "I'll run to the attic and grab that book I started a few days ago."

Walter hopped up after her as Dr. Fiske re-entered the room.

"Where are you two going?" he asked.

"Just to see if Lady Abigail needs help finding her book," Walter replied.

Miss Christiana snorted as Dr. Fiske shook his head.

Walter bounded up the stairs and entered their workspace just as Lady Abigail was crossing the room back towards the door again.

"Did you need something?" Abigail asked.

Walter gently touched the end of her hair. "Your hair is amazing. I adore it." He combed his fingers through it. "It's a shame you have to wear it up all the time."

Lady Abigail blushed again and stepped back. "We better go downstairs before Dr. Fiske gets fidgety."

Walter chuckled and then reached into his pocket. He handed her the tea invitation. "This for you from Mother."

Lady Abigail tore the note open. A wide smile spread across her face. "Your mother is inviting me to tea?"

Walter nodded.

"Thank you, Walter," she whispered, her eyes bright.

He tilted her chin and gave her a kiss. After pulling away, he gazed at her. "I'm falling in love with you, Abigail St. Clare."

She beamed at him. "Not like the first time?"

He grinned. "Nothing like the first time."

"And I might be head over heels for you, Walter Harding."

"That's definitely not like the first time," he teased.

She laughed and lightly hit his arm. "We should return."

Walter gave her a playful pout and reached for her. "Do we have to? We could stay up here, and you can play with numbers, and I can play with your hair..."

Abigail giggled and dodged him. As she walked by, she grabbed his hand, and the two headed back to the parlor.

******

Abigail exhaled as her carriage pulled up to the Harding home. It was somewhat ridiculous to ready the carriage for this trip; it was a short walk. But on a momentous occasion such as this, Abigail didn't want to leave anything to chance. She must look perfect and arrive in the best of style. *My relationship with Lord Darton might depend on it.*

She had been shocked and relieved to receive Lady Darton's invitation to tea. Hopefully, they could become better friends. Maybe Lord Darton was right, and all they needed was to become better acquainted with one another.

When the butler informed her tea would be in the
morning room, Abigail paused pulling off her gloves.
The morning room was a different mark of attention and
degree of familiarity she hadn't expected from Lady Darton. It was as though she were acknowledging Abigail's
soon-to-be family status. Abigail smiled, finished remov-
ing her things, and followed the butler into the morning
room.

It was an elongated octagonal shape and well lit, but
it wasn't excessively warm since the room wasn't in direct
sunlight. Large bay windows overlooked the garden,
and a service had been set up near the table by those
windows. It was a wonderful arrangement, and Abigail's
excitement increased. She curtsied low in front of Lady
Darton.

She nodded. "Lady Abigail."

"I thank you for your kind invitation to tea," said
Abigail.

"You're welcome, have a seat by the windows. I believe you'll enjoy the prospect."

Abigail smiled, trying not to appear giddy or over
eager as she took her seat. *It's so hard because I'm desperate
for this to go well.* "Indeed, I think I will."

Lady Darton poured their tea and told Abigail to
help herself to the selection of eats on the table.

Abigail took a biscuit and a sip of tea.

The two made light comments about the weather
and their respective gardens before they fell into silence.

"What is it about Dr. Fiske's house that's so fascinat-
ing?" Lady Darton asked. "From what Walter has vaguely
commented, I understand you're there with him and Dr.
Fiske quite often."

Abigail swallowed. "Dr. Fiske was my tutor. He's a
man of information, and I enjoy my discussions with
him."

Lady Darton raised an eyebrow. "And what is it that you discuss? I'm surprised a young lady such as yourself would have much to seriously consider with him."

Abigail studied Lady Darton for a moment. *I don't like the sound of that, and surely Walter has said enough that she should know better. I'll take a calculated risk.* "I'm a mathematician and do research in astronomy with Dr. Fiske and Lord Darton."

"A mathematician?" she repeated, her face blank.

Abigail narrowed her eyes. "Yes."

"You must forgive me. It's seldom that a noblewoman calls herself a mathematician."

"I'm no ordinary noblewoman." Abigail winced. *I'm supposed to play nice.*

"That's true," Lady Darton said wryly.

Abigail sighed. "Dr. Fiske gave me the same mathematics education a man would receive at university. He's used my calculations and work in a couple of papers he's written."

"I must warn you that ladies of society, especially young ladies, do not generally participate in such endeavors."

"I'm aware of that, and it's why I've been quiet about my work."

They ate and drank silently for a moment.

"You're welcome to stargaze with us anytime, Lady Darton," Abigail said quietly. "It's delightful."

Lady Darton stared at her. "I thank you for the invitation. But I don't think Walter would appreciate me intruding in his space in such a manner."

Abigail nodded. "If you ever wish to do so privately, I'd be very happy to share my love of astronomy with you."

Lady Darton bowed her head in a surprisingly gracious manner. "Thank you, Lady Abigail. That is kind of you."

The rest of tea was very agreeable. Abigail left about an hour later and smiled as she entered her carriage. *Maybe now I'm on my way to having a decent relationship with Lady Darton.*

CHAPTER 15

Showdown

Abigail

"You seem low in spirits today, Christiana," Abigail remarked as they took a leisurely walk. Abigail had just finished telling Christiana about tea with Lady Darton the day prior. And while Christiana was happy that the event appeared to be a success, she wasn't her usual enthusiastic self.

Christiana pulled a letter from her bag. "You might as well read this."

Abigail checked the signature at the bottom. "Your father couldn't speak the contents to you?"

"No, he spoke the contents," Christiana replied. "But being ever the businessman, he made sure to put it in writing too."

Abigail suppressed a chuckle, for she suspected the letter was rather serious.

Mr. Yeatman made it clear that if Christiana persisted in her present course towards engagement and marriage, she'd have no dowry and wouldn't be welcome in his home or society.

Abigail winced as she returned the letter. "I'm so sorry, my friend." She paused. "But surely you're not surprised by this?"

Christiana sighed. "No, I'm not. But to have his resolve on paper makes it very real and sobering."

"Have you shown Mr. Locke the letter?"

Christiana nodded.

"And what says he?" Abigail gently prodded.

"He wasn't surprised either," Christiana replied. "And to be honest, the news has less impact on him. He never expected a large dowry; I'm a huge exception. He's not in the same society as me now, so that's not a loss." She paused. "He doesn't like being unwelcome in my family, and he's very concerned about how this affects me."

The girls walked in silence for a moment.

"We argued," Christiana said. "He said maybe I shouldn't be attached to him."

"And what was your response?"

"I fought him on it. But you know what the horrible thing was?" Christiana's eyes were huge and glassy.

Abigail gave her an encouraging nod.

"I contemplated it." Christiana swiped her cheek. "How weak am I to contemplate giving up a man I love because it might be inconvenient for me?"

"This is far more than inconvenient, which is why Mr. Locke even mentioned it." Abigail stopped walking and took Christiana's hands in hers. "You'll be giving up your wealth, your station, and your family for a life with him. It's a huge sacrifice. He recognizes that and is concerned for your happiness."

"But I love him."

"I'm sure you do, tremendously. But like your mother said, day after day, year after year, this is the life you'll have. Just make sure you understand where you're landing before you leap."

"Yes, I see what you're saying." Christiana swiped her cheek again.

"Was the argument very bad?" Abigail asked gently.

"It was. But then there's so much at stake." Her voice cracked. "I don't know if we'll get through this one."

******

Walter

"A Mr. Edgar Locke requests an audience with you, sir," Walter's butler said to him in the library.

With a start, Walter looked up from some architectural plans. "I didn't even hear the door."

His butler gave him an odd look. "You wouldn't hear the back doors."

"He came through the back door?"

His butler stared at him. "Of course."

Walter shook his head. *I keep forgetting Locke's station.* In his mind, Edgar Locke was a gentleman. But while he's closer to the line than most, he was still very firmly servant class.

"Yes, please show him in," Walter replied.

Walter gave Locke a warm smile and motioned to the chair in front of his desk. "Please have a seat."

Locke shook his hand. "Thank you for seeing me like this, Lord Darton—"

"Just call me Harding. At least when we're alone like this or with Dr. Fiske."

"That'll take some getting used to for me."

Walter chuckled.

"I apologize for coming without a proper appointment," Locke said.

"Not at all. Something must be deeply troubling you to do so."

"Yes." He pressed his lips together. "I'm contemplating ending my courtship with Miss Yeatman."

On a certain level, Walter wasn't surprised. Locke was nothing if not responsible, and a marriage to Miss Christiana would, in many ways, sail in the face of that mindset. But on another level, Walter was disappointed for them. Their affection seemed very genuine, and Locke was a fine man.

"What are your reasons?" Walter asked.

He exhaled. "Miss Yeatman will give up so much. In the end, I don't know if being with me will be enough to compensate for that loss."

Walter winced. *That's a rather depressing assessment of his person. Possibly an accurate one, but bleak, nonetheless.* "Have you expressed this concern to Miss Christiana?" Walter asked.

"I have. And she, of course, fought me on it." He paused. "But for the first time, I saw a glimmer of doubt."

Walter nodded. "Do you think Miss Christiana incapable of adjusting to the life you lead?"

Locke's eyes widened. "No, not at all. Miss Yeatman is a force and capable of doing anything she puts her mind to. It's not her capacity I'm questioning; it's her long term happiness while doing it."

"Does she understand that?"

"What do you mean?"

"I can appreciate her hesitating in fully realizing everything she'd give up," Walter said. "If she didn't, I'd wonder at her."

Locke chuckled.

"But her doubt may have less to do with that and more to do with her uncertainty as to whether she'll make a good spouse for you," Walter explained. "The kind of concern you have for her happiness, she has for yours. And she may be less confident than you are in her capabilities to lead your life."

Locke shook his head. "I've never had any serious concerns along those lines. It'll be a major adjustment, but she's more than able to make it." He paused. "That perspective is not something I'd thought about. I'm glad you brought it to my attention."

"I'll say this, though I probably shouldn't." Walter paused. "While I'd completely understand ending your courtship with Christiana, it would sadden me seeing you two lose something special."

Locke's face softened. "Yes, that is most true."

******

Abigail

Abigail and Christiana came in from their walk and visit to the Upper Rooms a little somber. Usually, such an outing would brighten Christiana's mood, for she was quite popular and could always find ones to socialize with there. But people were a little cool towards her today. Abigail was sorry for it, but it could have been a lot worse. Perhaps they're waiting to see how far things would go with Mr. Locke.

They had made themselves comfortable in the drawing room when the butler announced that Lord Darton and Mr. Edgar Locke were there to call upon them.

Christiana and Abigail looked at one another in surprise. Christiana flushed and began fussing with her hair.

Abigail chuckled. "Look at you, all in a state because you're about to see your beau."

Christiana raised an eyebrow. "If you saw how pink your cheeks got and how bright your face glowed when Lord Darton was mentioned, you wouldn't say anything about me."

Abigail giggled.

Lord Darton and Mr. Locke were shown into the room.

Mr. Locke stopped short and beamed. "Christiana, I didn't know you'd be here."

She flew across the room and flung her arms around his neck. "I'm sorry for what I said and thought—"

Mr. Locke kissed her cheek. "Don't fret over that. But we do need a few moments conference in private, if that can be arranged?" He glanced at Abigail.

"Of course," she replied. "Why don't you two remain in here, and Lord Darton and I will be in either the morning room or library." Abigail smirked. "Wherever Mama and Papa are not."

Lord Darton chuckled.

They ended up in the library since her papa was out for the day.

"I'm quite astonished at this visit." She grinned. "Pleased though."

"Originally, we came to fetch you first and then come up with a scheme to get Miss Christiana," Lord Darton said. "If she's willing, and they work a few things out right now, Locke will ask for her hand in marriage."

Abigail gasped. "Mr. Yeatman will never give it."

"Locke realizes that, but he's going to ask anyway. When Mr. Yeatman refuses, they'll take the proper steps forward."

Abigail nodded and then smiled. "It seems you and he have become rather close."

Christiana burst into the room. Her eyes shone as she clutched Mr. Locke's hand. "Ready? Time for another visit to my father."

******

Walter

Mr. Yeatman was once again at the estate, so the four enjoyed another ride in the countryside. The mood was different on this trip. Miss Christiana and Locke seemed to be more united in purpose now.

When they entered her mansion, Mr. Locke told the butler he respectfully requested an audience with Mr. Yeatman.

Miss Christiana took Lady Abigail and Walter to the same room they waited in before, and then she plopped on the couch with a satisfied sigh. "This might be one of the last times I'm in here."

Walter nodded.

Lady Abigail looked between them. "You think it might become as bad as that?"

Miss Christiana let out a peal of laughter as Walter raised an eyebrow at Lady Abigail.

She reddened. "I suppose that was a rather obtuse statement given his previous behavior."

Locke entered the room.

"That was quick," Walter said.

He smirked as he sat beside Miss Christiana. "He refused to see me, so I gave him a letter of my own."

"Should we take our leave then?" Lady Abigail asked.

Locke shook his head. "I think he might have a change of heart in a moment."

A few minutes later, Mr. Yeatman burst into the room.

Locke rose from his seat and bowed. "Mr. Yeatman, I thank you for seeing me today."

Mr. Yeatman gave him a look. "Like I said, it's a shame you're courting my daughter. No wonder Lord Thurston hung onto you." He paused. "You may do what you like, Mr. Locke. But know that if you marry

Christiana, she'll have no dowry, no society, and she'll not be welcome here. I very clearly outlined those terms to her in writing."

"Yes, I saw the letter." Locke stared at Mr. Yeatman. "I'm asking Miss Yeatman for her hand in marriage. Are you sure this is the position you want to take?"

"It's the position she's forcing me to take," Mr. Yeatman replied.

He and Miss Christiana glared at one another.

Locke glanced between them. "We can live without the dowry and with the alteration in society. But I'm going to argue for her being welcome in your home. You don't have to welcome me, but please at least allow Miss Christiana to visit you and your wife once a year."

Mr. Yeatman stared hard at Miss Christiana. "This is not what I wanted."

Miss Christiana's face contorted as she opened her mouth.

Locke took her hand and gave her a very intense look. "Please," he said quietly.

Miss Christiana exhaled and took a step back.

Locke looked towards her father. "Please."

Mr. Yeatman crossed his arms. "Only because it would gratify her mother. And you might as well come too. I'd rather see you."

Christiana stepped forward, and Locke took her hand again. "Dear, please."

She nodded.

Locke exhaled. "Thank you, that's a better outcome than we'd anticipated, but we'll still leave here immediately. Is Miss Christiana allowed to return for her personal items?"

"Yes," Mr. Yeatman replied. "On a day of my choosing."

Locke nodded. "And is she still allowed to remain in her home in Bath?"

"Her mother and I won't be there, so go ahead."

Miss Christiana flinched.

"Our business is concluded, Mr. Locke." Her father gave him a curt nod.

Locke nodded back. "Mr. Yeatman."

Christiana's father walked towards the door, pausing at Walter and Lady Abigail. "I apologize for not greeting you properly earlier. Good afternoon, Lord Darton and Lady Abigail." He cast a final glance towards Miss Christiana and then walked out the door.

She deflated.

Locke rubbed her back. "I'm so sorry."

Miss Christiana shook her head. "Like you said, it went better than we thought it would." She grimaced. "Father gave you tacit consent. I just don't get anything."

He sighed. "Your father is a very odd man."

"You don't know the half of it," muttered Miss Christiana.

"Come, let's leave," Walter said gently.

They stopped at the same place they did on the previous trip.

"Are you two disappearing again?" Lady Abigail asked with a smirk.

Locke smiled. "No, this time I'd like for both of you to stay with us." He took Miss Christiana's hand, and Lady Abigail and Walter followed them to a little clearing in the woods by a stream.

"Give us a minute?" Locke asked.

Walter nodded and pulled Lady Abigail to him, as Locke led Miss Christiana to a rock and knelt before her.

"Yes! A thousand times, yes!" Miss Christiana exclaimed.

Lady Abigail shook her head.

Walter chuckled. "I sometimes wonder about your

friend."

Lady Abigail gave him a light smack on his stomach. "The same way I wonder about your Lord Thurston."

Walter laughed.

They watched as Locke said a few words to Miss Christiana that he couldn't quite make out. She threw her arms around his neck, and he kissed her and then held her for a moment. After they pulled apart, Miss Christiana waved them over.

Walter grabbed Lady Abigail's hand, and they walked towards the couple.

Locke had Miss Christiana by the waist, and she was glowing.

"We're engaged!" she exclaimed.

Lady Abigail dropped Walter's hand and crushed her in a hug.

Walter shook Locke's hand. "Let me know what you need help with, and I can try to assist you."

"You'd do that for me?" he asked in wonder.

Walter nodded. "I mean, I'm not buying you a house or anything—"

Locke laughed.

"But keep me in the know," Walter continued. "I feel this is harder than it should be, and I don't like that."

He nodded. "Thank you."

Walter slipped his hand into Lady Abigail's again, and the foursome strolled back to the carriage.

"Shall we head to Dr. Fiske's all together?" asked Walter. "Tell him the news?"

Miss Christiana nodded vigorously. "Maybe he has celebration pastries."

Locke kissed her cheek as Lady Abigail chuckled.

Walter shook his head. "I guess we can ask for those too." He squeezed Lady Abigail's hand. "Think you can get away with a little stargazing tonight?"

She smiled up at him. "Absolutely."

CHAPTER 16

Destroyed

Abigail

It was Friday, a week after Mr. Locke and Christiana had spoken with her father, and they became engaged. Christiana's parents had removed from their home in Bath at Mr. Yeatman's insistence. Mrs. Yeatman wasn't happy but hadn't voiced any substantial resistance. Abigail had helped Christiana pack her possessions in her country home, and Lord Darton and Mr. Locke had overseen the removal of her things to the house in Bath where she would live until the wedding.

All that activity had made for a busy week. The June weather was lovely, and she and Christiana had taken a walk in a park earlier that day. Abigail was able to work with Dr. Fiske for the first time that week, and she was in her usual happy spot at the desk in the attic, working on equations for Dr. Fiske's new conjectures and playing with her numbers.

She had seen Lord Darton only briefly this week when their paths had happened to cross while moving Christiana. She looked forward to spending more time with him today. Last Saturday was wonderful—

146

stargazing and spending time with the man she loved and her closest companions. A future filled with those kinds of days was just around the corner.

"Abigail, you need to read this," Dr. Fiske said with a quiet urgency she seldom heard from him.

Abigail looked up from her paper with a start and took the science journal from him. Her eyes widened as she read the article. "I can't believe this," she whispered.

The article was her and Lord Darton's work.

But her name was nowhere on it.

A sharp pain sliced through her body. "How could he do this to me?"

Dr. Fiske frowned. "I don't understand what happened. I can't believe Harding would do this. There must be some explanation."

Abigail sat back heavily in her chair, her mind in a fog. *I want to believe that.* She scanned the article again. *But I've spoken to no one about my work in this kind of detail, and Dr. Fiske's reaction indicates he hasn't either. Lord Darton must have done it.*

Abigail heard footfalls on the steps.

"Hello!" called Lord Darton.

It's bad enough my work was stolen, but I'm in love with the perpetrator...

He entered the attic, and her heart wrenched as she glanced at him. *I can't believe...* She put her head in her hands and leaned on the desk.

"Forecast says clear night tonight. We should get some good gazing—" There was a pause. "Whatever is the matter?"

Abigail listlessly handed the journal to Lord Darton.

He gasped. "How— What? How did this happen?"

"We hoped you could enlighten us," Dr. Fiske said quietly.

The room was engulfed in silence.

"I didn't have anything to do with this!" Lord Darton exclaimed. He tugged on Abigail's arm. "Abigail, I didn't do this!"

I can't... It hurts too much. "I have to go." She stood, reality a dream. *I must get out, make the pain stop.* "Lord Darton, I'm ending our courtship, and I don't want to ever see you again."

He paled. "Abigail, please believe me. I don't know how this happened—"

She shook her head. *He destroyed me. Again. Destroyed my work. Destroyed my trust. Everything important to me is crumbling...* She walked out of the room and out of the house.

How can I love a man who keeps doing this to me?

******

Walter

"Abigail!" Walter yelled and started after her.

Dr. Fiske yanked him back. "Let her go for now. She needs some space."

Walter stared at the door Abigail just walked through. *Let her go? I can't let her go.* He rubbed his chest as a sharp pain rented it. *How did this happen?*

"Do you know Lord Kengsley?" Dr. Fiske asked.

"Yes," replied Walter. "But I swear I never worked with him on anything. He's nothing more than an acquaintance."

"You never talked to him about your research?"

"Obliquely, but never in this kind of detail." Walter paced the room. *What happened?*

Dr. Fiske sighed. "How did he get this information? And why would he name you as a collaborator? If the man steals someone's work, you'd think he'd do it all the way."

Walter shook his head. "I don't know. I don't understand. And now Abigail—" He shoved himself into the chair she just vacated. "She ended us. I barely care about the research, but I can't lose her. And she believes I took her work. I would never—"

"Take a deep breath, Harding."

Walter inhaled.

"Try to think clearly," Dr. Fiske said. "For now, give Lady Abigail time to process the event. This is a massive blow to her in many ways. Anything you say right now will make the situation worse."

"You're right." He swallowed. "I have a better idea of how she felt when I ended our relationship without speaking to her." He closed his eyes as his shoulders sagged. "And now this. It's hopeless. She'll never want me back."

"Harding, focus," Dr. Fiske said. "Your chances will increase exponentially if you find out what really happened."

Walter opened his eyes and sat up straighter. "Yes." He looked at the journal and narrowed his eyes. "Who I need to speak with is Lord Kengsley."

Dr. Fiske nodded. "I think that's a much better idea."

Walter headed to the Upper Rooms since it was closest to Dr. Fiske's home and where he frequently ran into Lord Kengsley. To his relief, Lord Kengsley was there in the large octagonal shaped card room. Lady Edith was with him and two others at one of the card tables.

Lord Kengsley grinned. "Lord Darton! I thought I might see you today."

Walter glared at him. "What have you done? How dare you steal our work—"

A few people from other groups looked at them.

"You got almost all the credit," Lord Kengsley said. "I don't understand why you're so upset."

Walter got in his face. "Upset! You have no idea. You stole—"

"Temper, temper," Lord Kengsley chided. "You'll have us thrown out."

Walter growled but took a step back.

"We honestly did you a favor—" Lady Edith began.

Walter snapped his head towards her. *What did she do?* "We? A favor—"

Lord Kengsley put a hand up. "Hear us out."

He asked the others if they could postpone the start of the game a moment, and the Beaumont siblings and Walter walked out of the room to the gallery area.

"No one would believe those findings came from a woman," Lord Kengsley said.

Lady Edith shook her head. "I think Dr. Fiske assisted Lady Abigail a great deal." She chuckled. "He's probably half in love with her, so he let her take the credit. I don't understand why you put up with that. There are far more suitable ladies for a fine nobleman such as yourself."

Walter narrowed his eyes, his temperature rising. "Lady Abigail's work is all hers. She's a brilliant mathematician, and her contributions are a critical part of the research."

Lord Kengsley gave him a look.

"I resent the implication that there is anything inappropriate occurring between Dr. Fiske and Lady Abigail." Walter scowled at Lady Edith. "That was laid to rest long ago, and it's unladylike and vulgar to insist on bringing it up."

Lady Edith frowned as her face turned pink.

"As to why I so-called put up with her," Walter continued. "Lady Abigail is the finest woman in our set with superior intelligence and unparalleled beauty. I was fortunate she put up with me."

They stood in strained silence for a moment.

"As I said, no one will believe the computations were Lady Abigail's doing," Lord Kengsley said. "Your work would've been dismissed. This way it'll receive the attention it deserves."

"You had no right to make that call," Walter snapped. "I don't understand why you'd insert yourselves in my business this way."

Lord Kengsley raised an eyebrow. "I'm surprised you're not more grateful. Lady Abigail can continue working with you, and now you have some real traction in the astronomy field."

Walter scoffed. "Grateful? You stole our work, deleted Lady Abigail's involvement, destroyed our relationship—"

Lord Kengsley's eyes lit up. "Ah, now we get closer to the point. So, she didn't take kindly to this, not that I blame her."

"What kind of wife would she have made you anyway?" Lady Edith asked. "Lady Darton never approved of her goings-ons."

Walter stilled. "What does my mother have to do with this?"

Lady Edith smiled. "Probably more than you'll ever want to believe." Her face hardened. "She and I are both of the mind that Lady Abigail needs to be brought down a few pegs. She acts with the airs of royalty and has nothing to back it up. She even spurned dear Kengsley's attentions for no good reason." She scowled. "As if a marquess wasn't good enough for her."

As if Lady Abigail would consider only the station and not the man behind it. A flash of heat traveled through Walter's body. He fought the urge to berate Lady Edith again because he couldn't persist in doing that no matter how much it was deserved.

She gave him a coy smile. "But you're perfectly suitable for the daughter of a marquess. I know Lady Darton would have no qualms with that. The daughter of a marquess who knows how to act like a proper lady."

It's time to reacquaint her with reality... "There is nothing in your present behavior that is ladylike," Walter retorted. "I cannot stress enough how impossible it'd be for me to be connected with any woman who acts in a manner such as this."

Lady Edith paled.

Walter remembered what she had said about his mother, and his temperature dropped as sharply as it had risen. *That can't be true. There's no way my mother could be involved with this.*

He narrowed his eyes at them. "Understand, unequivocally, how furious I am over your actions. If I see your name with mine again, I'll do anything necessary to destroy that connection."

"That's fair enough, I suppose, if you feel it's necessary," said Lord Kengsley.

Walter gave him a curt nod and walked away. He thundered into his carriage and rubbed his face. *I can't believe they did this.*

******

Abigail

Abigail sat in the bay window in the morning room, finishing her needlepoint project. Lord Darton had written and requested the privilege of her audience. She sent a note stating there could be no explanation for what he did and to please not contact her further.

It was hard enough working through this. There were times when she felt as though she were about to lose her mind, and she didn't need him to push the knife further. To try to take her mind off him, Abigail had volunteered to go to the orphanage for Lady Broughton since she had suddenly taken ill and present the proceeds from the first batch of pieces sold.

Abigail looked out at the garden and frowned, remembering her pleasant afternoon tea with Lady Darton. *I wonder if she's happy things are at an end between Lord Darton and me.*

"Abigail?" Mama asked.

She snapped her head towards her. "Yes?"

"I called you three times. Will you attend the Venetian breakfast with me?"

"Yes, of course," Abigail replied and directed her attention back to her needlework again. But a few moments later, she looked out the window again and watched the first splatters of rain hit the glass. *Even this reminds me of Lord Darton — the day he gave me the tea invitation. His fingers in my hair. And that kiss...*

I can't seem to get away from him. Everything I do brings memories that then pain me. He told me he was falling in love with me. How could he say that and then do this? Her chest felt like it was cracking again, and she winced.

"Abigail, dear, is something the matter?" Mama asked softly. "You haven't been yourself the last few days. I know I'm always speaking to you about being demure, but I don't want you to be lifeless either. It's not you."

Abigail attempted to give her a courageous smile but couldn't. A huge lump formed in her throat.

Mama sat next to her on the bay window seat. "It's Lord Darton, isn't it?" she asked and put her arms around Abigail. "And it's more than an argument. It's happened this time, didn't it? Your heart is hurting?"

Abigail nodded and stared out the window giving her cheek an angry swipe. "He stole my work."

"He what?" Mama asked.

"He published our work and didn't give me credit. I trusted him." Abigail's voice hitched. "I loved him. And he did this to me."

"I'm so sorry, Abigail, and quite astonished. I thought the affection was true this time and mutual. Are you quite certain he did this?"

Abigail nodded violently. "I read the article. My math. My conclusions. In black and white. With my name nowhere near. Only Lord Darton's name and Lord Kengsley, who had nothing to do with anything."

Mama frowned. "I admit I don't quite understand, but obviously it's important. What did Lord Darton have to say for himself?"

Abigail snorted. "That he didn't do it."

The room grew quiet.

"Have you considered that maybe he didn't?" Mama asked.

"Of course, he did something!" Abigail exclaimed and started pacing in front of the window. "The information didn't just magically appear in the journal, and it's not like we showed everyone our work and calculations."

"Yes, I can understand that." Mama bit her lip. "Just be careful not to make the same mistake he did with you a few months ago."

Abigail stopped pacing and crossed her arms. *Mama's words ring true, but I don't want to hear them now.* "You were right. It was all tomfoolery. I should have never thought I could do this."

Mama's face fell. "Abigail, I never wanted—"

"No one will take me seriously. And I handed my heart over to a man just so he could stab me in the back—"

"I think you should—"

"I'm done. With all of it. From now on, I'll act as a

proper countess. I'll make a match that's proper but not emotional. I'll take my place in society as society dictates."

Mama sighed.

Abigail picked up her needlepoint, sat primly on the couch, and resumed her work.

******

Walter

Dr. Fiske's face lit up as Walter stepped into his study. "Harding! What do you have there?"

"I'm bringing you my telescope," replied Walter.

Dr. Fiske's face fell. "Don't do this—"

"I must. I can't—" Walter closed his eyes. "Every time I try, I think of her, and I can't do it anymore."

"She'll come round, Harding."

Walter shook his head. "You heard her. She doesn't want to see me again. She refuses to see me when I call and has returned all my letters — the ones I just sent were unopened and all my old ones. I'm fortunate she didn't ask me for hers back."

Dr. Fiske winced.

Walter patted his telescope. "This is too fine a scope to leave to waste, so I'm giving it to you."

Dr. Fiske stared at him a moment. "Your father's telescope?"

Walter nodded and tried to smile at him. "Father would've liked you. I think he would have approved."

Dr. Fiske shook his head. "Harding, I can't—"

"Please do this for me," Walter said quietly.

Dr. Fiske nodded though he still didn't look happy.

Walter pulled the legs out and placed it gently on the floor. "I can think of no better home." He exhaled and clapped his hands. "Now, it's time for me to be an actual earl." He gave a half-hearted laugh. "I don't know what I was thinking, imagining I could be in the scientific arena."

"It's not like you failed in your endeavor."

"I failed in the most important endeavor." Walter's heart twisted. "I can't participate in something that causes so much devastation." He held out his hand. "I'm leaving for London again. Dr. Fiske, I'll never forget my time with you. You're a true and trusted friend."

Dr. Fiske gave him a wan smile and shook his hand. "As you are mine. You're always welcome here, and your spot will remain, astronomer or not."

Walter nodded. "Thank you." He tipped his hat and walked out of the study and out of the house.

CHAPTER 17

Astronomers

Walter

It was mid July, and Walter was in an assembly room in London awaiting a talk by a member of an astronomy society. He had just finished an appointment with Lord Manton, who took the property and would also meet with Walter in the future to look at agricultural property in Bath. Walter had no idea what he was up to.

Despite his declaration that he was through with astronomy, his curiosity had gotten the better of him when he'd seen the announcement. *I guess I can't give it up for keeps.*

Walter looked around and swallowed. *Brings back memories... Abigail would have loved to hear this.*

He blinked, not believing what he was seeing and crossed the room. "Dr. Fiske!" he exclaimed and pumped his hand. "It's great to see you here! What brings you to London?"

Dr. Fiske smiled. "You."

"Me?"

"Yes, I was hoping to run into you." He handed Walter an invitation. "I've been asked to speak at a lecture in Bath. I wanted to invite you." He gave him a wry smile. "I'll need the support. I'm not one for public speaking."

Walter's smile broadened. "That's excellent. I'll make arrangements to be there unless something dire happens here."

"Thank you."

"Not that I don't enjoy seeing you, but this could have been sent post instead of hand delivered."

Dr. Fiske's eyes bore into his. "You need to resume your work."

Walter shook his head sharply. "No. I'm done with that." *I knew coming here would make that issue rear its ugly head. I just didn't think it'd come in the form of Dr. Fiske.*

The doctor gave him a look. "You can't even stay away. Look at you; you're here."

Walter exhaled. *He's got me there.* "I should have never been involved in the first place. I'm a nobleman, an earl. It's time I act as such."

"You can be an astronomer and still be nobleman."

"I can't..." Walter rubbed his face. "It destroyed what I care about most."

"It also gave you what you care about most."

Walter stared at him. *He's right. Without astronomy, Abigail and I wouldn't have had another chance.*

"Make this right, Harding," Dr. Fiske said quietly. "Come back." He clapped Walter's shoulder. "Now follow me. I have fine seats."

Is it too late? Can I make things right?

******

Abigail

"Lady Abigail, Dr. Fiske is here to call on you," the butler said Saturday morning.

Abigail stilled, dropping her needlework on her lap. *Dr. Fiske rarely calls on people.* She cleared her throat. "You can show him in."

A moment later, Dr. Fiske walked into the drawing room and smiled warmly at her. "Lady Abigail, it's very good to see you."

"Yes, this is a pleasant surprise. Please make yourself comfortable. What can I do for you?"

Dr. Fiske gave her an invitation to hear him speak, and Abigail enthusiastically assured him she'd be there.

His smile faded a little. "Come back."

Abigail looked away. "I can't." *I want to. I miss it so much. But I can't...* She blinked.

"Lord Darton did not give your work away," Dr. Fiske said gently.

"How can you be so sure?" she asked, still not meeting his eyes.

"He was just as shocked as you were and has since quit the scientific sphere."

Abigail whipped her head around. "What?" *He wouldn't publish such a paper only to leave. Mama's words — maybe Lord Darton was telling the truth. And I wouldn't listen.*

"Harding has left astronomy," Dr. Fiske repeated. "He even gave me his telescope."

"He can't do that. It was the scope he and his father used."

Dr. Fiske gave her a weak smile. "I know."

Abigail exhaled. *He shouldn't give up something so precious...*

"He hasn't been back to research since the day he read the article," Dr. Fiske said. "Further, I spoke with his so-called collaborator, and Harding hasn't seen Lord Kengsley since that same day. Harding was livid and told him in very strong terms to keep his distance. Lord Kengsley and his sister acted unilaterally and without his consent."

Lady Edith? How is she involved? Abigail wrinkled her brow. "Then how did they—"

"I don't know all the mechanics," Dr. Fiske said. "But I've just returned from London where I saw Harding. He's heartbroken, as I believe and can understand you are."

Abigail swallowed and looked away again. *I've made a massive mistake. How do I mend things? Can I?*

"Neither one of you can give it up completely," said Dr. Fiske. "I found him at an astronomy lecture." He gave her a wry smile. "And your needlepoint is quite stellar."

Despite herself, Abigail chuckled. The woman she'd spoken with at Lady Broughton's party had designed an excellent but complicated moon, stars, and flowers design at Abigail's request.

"The two of you make a wonderful team, in many ways," said Dr. Fiske. "Please, come back, Lady Abigail. I miss my friends. It's rather lonely doing this by myself. I don't know how I managed it before meeting the two of you."

I don't know how to correct matters with Lord Darton, but I can start with this. Abigail smiled. "I'll come back, Dr. Fiske."

******

Walter

Walter took a deep breath as he stood on Dr. Fiske's doorstep. It was mid August, about a month from when he had seen Dr. Fiske in London. His time there had concluded, so he was back in Bath and would return to Darton for the fall and winter within the week.

The last time I was here — his heart twisted as Lady Abigail's face floated through his mind. This will be a rough afternoon. He swallowed. *I'm here to support Dr. Fiske while he gives his lecture.* Walter turned the doorknob and walked into the house. "Hello!" he called out.

"In here, Harding," Dr. Fiske responded.

Walter walked to the parlor and froze at the door.

Abigail stared at him from the couch with her clear gray eyes.

I can't believe she's here.

"I'll give you two a few moments alone together." Dr. Fiske walked out of the room.

"You're back," Lady Abigail whispered.

Walter nodded, his heart slamming his chest. *I can't find the words... So much to say...*

"It's good to see you," she said. "You're here for Dr. Fiske's lecture as well?"

Walter nodded again. *Dr. Fiske must have arranged this. He must think Abigail's feelings towards me have changed at least a little...*

Silence.

Say something. Walter took a deep breath. "How have you been, Lady Abigail?"

She shrugged. "I've been better." She paused. "I suppose you heard Lady Broughton died quite suddenly?"

"Yes, I did," Walter replied. "That was very upsetting news." Lady Broughton fell ill and was dead two weeks later. "I heard her husband and daughter are devastated."

Lady Abigail nodded. "I called on Miss Portia after it happened, and I've taken over Lady Broughton's charity needlepoint project in her name." She looked down. "It keeps me occupied now that I don't—" she exhaled.

"I never breathed a word about your work to—"

"I know," she said.

"I want to be partners."

Abigail nodded. "That's partially why I came back—"

"In every way."

She stilled, her eyes going wide.

"I love you," Walter said. "I can't do what we just did again. It killed me to be apart from you."

Abigail's mouth opened slightly.

He swallowed. "I'm sorry. We can just hear Dr. Fiske speak today and support him. I didn't mean to make you uncomfortable—"

"I love you too."

Walter reached for a nearby chair to keep him standing and then grinned. "Truly?"

Lady Abigail smiled back. "Truly."

"We're back again?"

"Yes, we're back." She laughed. "For the third time."

"Try, try, and try again, I think is how the old saying goes." *She's here. We're together. This is unbelievable...* "Can I kiss you?"

Abigail rolled her eyes. "You and the asking. It's so odd—"

Walter crossed the room in two steps and had his hands on the side of her face, kissing her like his life depended on it. He finally pulled away and gazed at her.

Lady Abigail grabbed his hands. "Walter, I'm so sorry I didn't believe you, trust you—"

"I understand, and it doesn't matter now. As long as we don't do this again. You have no idea how gutted I was."

"Me too," she whispered.

"Should we find Dr. Fiske?" Walter asked. "He'll be ready to leave shortly."

Lady Abigail nodded.

Walter pulled her from the couch, and hand in hand they went to find Dr. Fiske.

*****

Abigail

He loves me. Abigail had no idea today would turn out like this, and she couldn't stop smiling. Dr. Fiske hadn't told her Lord Darton was coming, and she had assumed he was still in London.

Dr. Fiske's grimace turned into a grin when they entered his study. "I take it you two worked something out?"

Abigail and Lord Darton exchanged smiles.

"Yes, Dr. Fiske, we've definitely reached an understanding." Walter squeezed her hand. "But you don't seem happy. Are you nervous for your talk? I'm sure you'll do fine."

Dr. Fiske's grimace returned. "This was so disturbing I'd forgotten about the talk." He handed a journal to Lord Darton. "I believe I may have a spy here."

Abigail looked over his shoulder at the article and wrinkled her brow. "It's the work you and I did together on the minor planet. I wonder why they bothered printing it."

"Independent verification is important and will garner those involved some recognition. I was going to encourage you to publish your findings eventually. It was just your work with Walter was taking off, so I figured I'd wait." Dr. Fiske frowned. "It appears that was unwise."

"I'd find it hard to believe the Beaumonts have physically been here," said Lord Darton. "Who's getting all this information and how?"

"That's the question," Dr. Fiske said. "I'll interrogate my staff. I have a feeling someone may be slipping information or allowing another party unauthorized access."

Abigail's eyes widened. "That's very serious."

"It is. I never believed anyone here would be so disloyal." Dr. Fiske was quiet a moment. "I know it's hard for you to hear, Harding, but—"

Walter closed his eyes. "You think my mother may have something to do with this."

"I do," he said quietly. "I have no real evidence to back that belief, so I may be speaking grossly out of turn. But it's interesting that these attacks specifically wound Abigail."

She ran a hand over her forehead. "Our time at tea was so encouraging. Why does she hate me so? What have I done to her?"

Dr. Fiske grimaced. "I don't know. But I suggest you find out because she seems bent on ruining your life for some reason."

"When I saw the Beaumonts, they told me Mother never approved of Lady Abigail's so-called goings-ons and that she had more to do with this than I'd want to believe." Lord Darton shook his head. "I have to stop ignoring what's in front of me."

"Do you know why your mother is so violently against Lady Abigail?" Dr. Fiske asked. "Lady Edith and Lord Kengsley I could make some conjectures about; I assume that's from a romantic standpoint."

Abigail cringed. "Lord Kengsley did take an interest in me when I first entered society, but I just couldn't..." she exhaled.

Lord Darton smiled. "I perfectly understand."

"I thought I discouraged things appropriately." She gave them a wry smile. "I guess not."

Dr. Fiske chuckled. "Rejection is rejection, no matter how gently it's done.

Lord Darton nodded. "Lord Kengsley isn't one to take it well. He's used to doing the rejecting." He paused. "As for Lady Edith..."

"She's never liked me." Abigail smirked. "I'm sure she was overjoyed to hear our engagement came to an end and then most exasperated to hear our courtship began anew." She squeezed his hand. "You're quite the catch.

"That doesn't explain my mother's behavior though," said Lord Darton. "It's one thing to oppose my engagement to a girl she believed had an outside relationship. This is far more extreme and malicious, not to mention premeditated. I can't fathom why she's acting in this manner." He looked at Abigail. "But I think it's time we find out."

Abigail raised an eyebrow.

"Will you accompany me to call on Mother tomorrow?" he asked with a wry grin.

Abigail gave him a wan smile back. "I will."

"Now, enough talk about this," Lord Darton said. "Let's depart for Dr. Fiske's lecture where we will cheer him on."

"Will you two come back afterward for dinner and stargazing?" Dr. Fiske asked. "I'll need something to ease my agitation afterward."

Abigail nodded enthusiastically.

"Agitation? This is your triumph." Lord Darton grinned. "Your time in glory."

Dr. Fiske gave him a look.

Walter chuckled. "Of course, we'd be happy to share a celebratory dinner and stargazing session."

Dr. Fiske smiled and stood. "Now I'm ready."

CHAPTER 18

Thorns and Fire

Walter

Walter had asked Dr. Fiske if he'd accompany them to see his mother. She had removed from their town house in Bath to Darton, at the end of June when he had left for London. Walter was quiet while the three of them rode in his barouche to his estate the next day. *I can't fathom why Mother would want to make Lady Abigail's life so miserable. It's senseless.*

But she is, and I must come to grips with that. Lady Abigail will never be happy in a marriage with me if Mother is attacking and undermining her all the time. I hope she won't issue any ultimatums...

"This is your first time to Darton, isn't it?" Walter asked Lady Abigail.

She nodded.

Walter grimaced. "I wish it were under better circumstances."

Dr. Fiske raised an eyebrow at them. "It's a wonder it hasn't happened before. How long were you two engaged?"

"Four months," replied Lady Abigail. "But it was over the winter, and the wedding wasn't until May." She shrugged. "I figured I'd see it during the spring."

Dr. Fiske shook his head and chuckled. "You two are so odd."

Walter and Lady Abigail grinned at one another.

Her eyes widened as they pulled to the front of Harding Court. "I heard Darton was a great estate, but now seeing it..." she trailed off.

Walter grinned, puffing his chest out a bit and resisting the urge to thump it. *I'm glad my lady likes my place.* Harding Court was a square building constructed of golden colored stones with an enclosed courtyard. It was nestled in a valley with tree laden hills on one side and a nearby lake on the other. The grounds were well kept but simple giving the estate a sharp and pleasant appearance.

The butler informed Walter that his mother was working on her correspondence in the drawing room as he took their things.

"Please inform her we respectfully require an audience with her," Walter turned. "Ready?" he asked Lady Abigail and Dr. Fiske.

They nodded, and the three were shown into the drawing room.

Lady Darton sat ramrod straight in her chair with a cane in hand situated in front of the bowed wall of windows that offered a view of the lake beyond.

Ever the queen.

Walter crossed the room and kissed the cheek she offered. "Hello, Mother."

"Good morning, Walter. What is it that you require?" she asked.

"Don't you want to greet our visitors first?" asked Walter with an edge.

"Lady Abigail, Dr. Fiske," his mother said coolly.

They greeted her in return, and then she raised an eyebrow at him.

"What is your grievance against Lady Abigail?" Walter asked quietly.

Her face went blank. "Grievance? I don't know what you're—"

"Mother, don't patronize me right now." His voice was still quiet, but it was firm. "What is your grievance against Lady Abigail?"

Lady Darton stared at him a moment. "I think this is the first time I've seen you show some backbone, Walter."

He glared at her. *Remember, she is my mother. I love my mother...*

The Dowager Darton stared towards Lady Abigail, her eyes going a cold gray, like bullets.

Abigail's breathing picked up, and Walter took her hand.

"The St. Clares have been a thorn in my side for the last twenty-five years," said his mother as she stared towards Lady Abigail.

She squeezed his hand. "Why?"

"We'll begin with your mother, the always formidable Lady Mary Anne, perfect woman of society."

Lady Abigail's eyes widened.

"Ever since I was fourteen, all I ever heard was what perfection Lady Mary Anne was." His mother twisted her face. "My own mother was constantly singing her praises and holding her out as a model for me." She smirked at Lady Abigail. "How would you like it if your mother told you to be more like Lady Edith?"

Lady Abigail made a face.

"We know what a big fan of Lady Edith you are," Walter said. "She told me that you thought she was a better partner for me."

His mother scowled. "I thought no such thing. Where would she ever get that idea?"

Walter gave her a look. "Perhaps your willingness to make her an accomplice in your intrigues against Lady Abigail?"

Lady Darton shrugged. "I suppose that could give one some false hope. But her overeagerness to participate would automatically take her out of the running. To have such a girl as a daughter-in-law..." She shuddered. "Besides, I absolutely can't abide her voice."

Walter shook his head. *Mother is a piece of work.* "You're telling me you tried to destroy Lady Abigail's work and our relationship because my grandmother kept telling you to be more like Lady Mary Anne?"

Lady Darton glared at him. "You don't understand. It was everything she supposedly embodied. This is how a true woman of society is supposed to behave, and how I'd never be one because I loved chemistry."

Lady Abigail gasped.

Walter's jaw dropped. "What?"

"You never knew I tried to study chemistry, did you?" Lady Darton asked.

Walter stared at his mother. "Of course not. You never mentioned it."

"I was told no lady of society can go on about such things and was forced to give it up," she said. "The closest I'd come to science was looking at the stars with you and your father."

"I'm sure he would have—"

"Don't be simple, Walter," she snapped. "In hindsight, he might have let me dabble. But my place was sounded down in me before I married, and I'm pretty sure your father wouldn't have strayed far from it." Lady Darton set her jaw as she glared at Lady Abigail. "Why should she get to study and pursue her passion when I could not?"

"Mother, I'm sure—" he began.

"You're sure what?" his mother asked. "That it's not true? That people would never act in such a manner? Say such things?" She gave a nasty laugh. "I'm not good enough for society, but Lady Mary Anne's daughter is?" She stood abruptly. "Her daughter, who is praised as much or even more than Lady Mary was, but is carrying on in the streets, abandoning every rule of decorum—"

Lady Abigail cringed.

"Mother!" Walter exclaimed.

"No!" his mother yelled. "You listen to me. I'm done sitting by watching the hypocrisy." She pointed at Abigail. "I'll expose this woman for the farce that she is."

"You're quite right, Lady Darton," said Lady Abigail

His mother stopped short.

Lady Abigail squared her shoulders and dropped Walter's hand. "I'll stop doing my research in secret. I'll publish my articles, seek to get in on lectures, and speak about my work with pride, accepting the consequences, whatever they may be." She narrowed her eyes. "But if you ever attempt to destroy my reputation again by means of slander, you'll reckon with me; and remember, I have no problems abandoning every so-called rule of decorum, as you stated."

Dr. Fiske snorted behind them.

Lady Darton's eyes widened.

Abigail took a step forward. "My mother puts on a genteel act, but she'll be the first to tell you I'm not my mother's daughter, and I have no qualms being things other than genteel," Abigail continued. "I don't believe you're ready to expose this farce because I have serious doubts you'll be able to withstand my fire. Have I made my position clear?"

"Crystal," Lady Darton replied in a clipped tone.

The room filled with silence.

"You must stop, Mother," Walter said quietly.

"And you'll abandon your own mother?" she asked.

"I'm not abandoning you, but you must stop this behavior," Walter answered. "It's beneath you; this isn't you. Did you honestly expect Lady Abigail to make it known that she's engaging in scientific research? What course of action did you expect her to take?"

His mother looked away towards the window.

"Lady Abigail and I are continuing our work as partners," said Walter.

His mother stared at him a moment. "I'm trying to decide if you're willingness to buck the order in this regard is due to naivety or if you have more gumption than I ever gave you credit for."

"If that is the so-called order, then yes, I believe it should change," he said.

"And you're willing to lead that charge?" Lady Darton smirked.

Walter gave her an even look. "Are you forcing me to charge against you?" He paused. "I love you, and I won't abandon you, Mother, unless you press the issue. Please don't force me to choose between you and my wife because you'll not come out the victor."

Mother and son stared at one another for a moment.

"But I'd rather have your support and help. Please build us up instead of tearing us down." He approached her and tried to kiss her cheek, but she turned her head slightly.

He grimaced and patted her hand. "We'll take our leave now. Goodbye, Mother."

The three solemnly exited the room.

"I didn't know how much in common your mother and I have," Lady Abigail said. "I wish we could have been friends instead of at odds with one another."

"I'm hoping you two will still be friends," Walter said. "I know she's shown you an ugly side, but I've seen her capable of great good. I just wish she hadn't let this wound fester to the degree that it was toxic to her."

Lady Abigail exhaled. "Not that I condone her behavior, but it's hard, Lord Darton. I don't know if you understand how frustrating it is to be in our position."

Walter shook his head as they waited in the entryway for the carriage. "I don't, not truly. I felt it was unusual for someone in my position to pursue such things, but it's not as though anyone has tried to stop me."

Lady Abigail put a hand on Walter's arm. "I never wanted to drive a wedge between you and your mother." She gave him a rueful smile. "Despite all the things I've said in the past about you being unable to stand up to her."

"I should have paid heed sooner. I might have been able to stop the sequence of events before they got so out of hand." He sighed. "She'll come round."

The three entered the barouche.

"I'll hope for the best then," said Abigail.

CHAPTER 19

Diamond in the Sky

Abigail

Lord Darton's carriage pulled in front of a farm. A tenant farmer on Lord Thurston's estate was happy to lend it as the site for Mr. Locke and Christiana's wedding and festivities.

"Locke wouldn't let me pay for another venue," said Walter.

Abigail smiled at him and patted his hand.

"This will probably be more enjoyable," Dr. Fiske said from across the carriage. "I wager his guests would feel uncomfortable at some fancy place like the Upper Rooms."

Walter nodded. "I suppose so."

Dr. Fiske chuckled. "I imagine your presence will already make a splash."

"I hope not." Abigail grimaced. "I don't want to take away from their day."

Abigail knew that the three of them were the only ones of Christiana's old society who would be here. She had received some comments about her intentions on attending. Christiana had stopped receiving invitations after her engagement to Mr. Locke and her father's public disapproval.

Fortunately, Mr. Locke's friends had received her well. Christiana said at first, they were concerned that she'd force him to somehow keep up the life she had known. They loved him and looked on him as a leader in their own society. But when she had asked for help in learning specific tasks, the women had welcomed the requests and her with open arms.

Abigail glanced at Walter. "Did Lord Thurston mention whether he'll attend?"

"I believe he may stop by later, perhaps with a small gift," Walter replied. "But no, I don't believe he was participating."

Abigail nodded. "He's not in favor then?"

"He's not against the marriage," Walter replied. "But he has his limits, and socializing with his servants and employees is one of them. As Locke said, Thurston is always very much master."

"Mr. Locke did take me up on borrowing my French chef, probably at Christiana's pleas," Dr. Fiske said.

Walter grinned. "Excellent."

The footmen handed them out of the carriage.

"Christiana had asked me to help her prepare, so I hope you men will find some way to occupy yourselves." Abigail raised an eyebrow.

A young woman, with startlingly sky-blue eyes, approached Lady Abigail and curtsied. "I believe you're Lady Abigail St. Clare?"

"I am." Abigail scrutinized her. "You're the woman from the orphanage."

She nodded. "I was asked if I could be spared today to help for a small wage."

When Abigail had visited the orphanage with the funds, the headmistress had been gone for the day taking care of necessary business, and this young woman had cared for her needs. She was quiet but very capable, with a restful quality that Abigail had appreciated at the time. Due to Lady Broughton's recent death, the errand had been more emotional than she had anticipated.

"Miss Christiana asked that I bring you to her when you arrived, milady," the young woman said.

"I'll let you lead the way then." Abigail followed her inside a small but pleasant cottage. "What's your name?" Abigail asked. *She seems out of place, both here and at the orphanage, like she's caught between worlds.*

The young woman turned. "I'm Hannah Northrop."

"There's lots of activity and laughter." Abigail grinned. "That's as it should be."

Miss Northrop smiled as she started up the stairs. "I believe Miss Christiana makes laughter easy."

"Abigail!" Christiana exploded from the side of the bed in a small room and gave Abigail a monstrous hug.

Abigail held her arm's length. "Have you done anything to prepare yourself?"

"Ugh," groaned Christiana. "It's so hard without my lady's maid. I never realized how dependent I was on her. It took three times as long to do things, and I still look the worse for all the work."

"I'm glad I told mine to come," Abigail said.

Christiana squealed. "You did?"

Abigail smiled. "She should be here any minute now. The servant's wagon wasn't far behind ours. Lord Darton and I decided we'd bring some help, so your guests can celebrate with you."

Christiana hugged her tight again. "Thank you! You are the bestest friend in the whole wide world."

There was a knock on the door, and her lady's maid entered with another young girl, and the three got down to the business of making Christiana look like a bride.

****

The wedding was a very different affair from any Abigail had ever attended.

As they were eating, Lord Darton smiled at her. "Are you well?"

She exhaled and put her fork down. "I'm trying to relax so I'm not seen as a snob."

"You've been friendly," Lord Darton said. "I don't think anyone sees you as anything other than Christiana's good friend."

Abigail grimaced. "I'm trying, but I'm having difficulty finding my footing. I feel like I'm extra cool and reserved." She snorted. "I always saw myself as a rebel, of sorts. I guess I really am shaped by my society."

Dr. Fiske smiled at her. "You're fine, Abigail. Enjoy the food and your friends."

The food was quite good. Different from her typical fare and a little heavy, but still tasty. And the French treats were yet to come.

After eating, the dancing began, and Abigail enjoyed watching the merrymaking. Christiana was a beautiful and gracious bride, and she didn't seem set apart from everyone else. Mr. Locke beamed as though he were the sun. At this moment, people were happy, and they weren't shy about showing it, which was a refreshing change.

Several hours later, after some of the guests had left, Christiana took a seat next to Abigail.

"Tell me about your new home," Abigail said.

"Lord Thurston told Edgar that if he was considering renting a cottage, he'd rather it be on his land so he could get the rent," said Christiana.

Abigail laughed.

"He made improvements on the steward's old

cottage for Edgar, negotiated a low rent, and threw in several acres of land," Christiana continued. "We had considered buying a small plot of land, but we think this will be easier for us, at least in the beginning."

"It sounds like a good arrangement."

"Yes, it's pretty and quaint, but it'll take some getting used to for me. I'm already at a loss with so little help. Edgar says we'll keep two people for now — a man and a woman to help with the house and cook. In time we should be able to slowly hire others."

The move on Edgar's part to get a cook might just save their marriage. "Mr. Locke seems to be a very good man."

Christiana grinned. "He's absolutely wonderful. The best." She hugged Abigail. "I'm sad that we won't be in one another's society any longer."

"We'll still be the closest of friends." Abigail grabbed her hand and squeezed it. "I'll come and visit, and you're welcome to see me."

"Yes, you're always welcome in our home." Christiana kissed Abigail's cheek and hugged her once more.

******

Walter

Walter had invited Abigail, Dr. Fiske, and the Lockes to visit Darton for a few days towards the end of September. Dinner had been eaten, and now the group was in his observatory. A fire was going in the room, and they had wine, some fine pastries, and made snacks of toasted bread with melted cheese in the fire.

Dr. Fiske was at the scope. "I love looking at the sky here. So much more to see than from my attic window."

Walter agreed, but then Dr. Fiske's attic provided so much more in terms of mental stimulation. *And it gave me Abigail back.* He glanced at her.

Abigail was standing not too far from him, looking out a different window with the spyglass he had given her, cheeks flushed and looking as lovely as Walter had ever seen her. She had just published her first solitary paper about the confirmation of the minor planet sighting. She'd only heard from a couple of other astronomers, but their responses were encouraging as her math was much more in-depth than the initial report.

Abigail grinned at him. "It's nice that your mother joined us for a little bit."

After his mother came to grips with the fact that he was madly in love with Abigail, she came around, proving Walter right, and was endeavoring to be civil towards her. She had apologized to Abigail for any undue damage she might have done to her reputation. However, she had backhandedly intimated that there wasn't any permanent harm done because she was a St. Clare, and of course, the St. Clare's were untouchable. Abigail, being the lady that she was, let the comment slide.

Dr. Fiske had interrogated his staff and discovered Lady Darton had been paying the head housekeeper to give her information. The revelation had rocked Dr. Fiske, as he thought the housekeeper was a good worker, and he realized she could have been using other servants to gather information. Dr. Fiske decided to let the entire staff go, except his chefs, and carefully hire new, as it would be safer for him. The ones he suspected were innocent, he gave good references and helped secure other decent positions.

Walter was appalled. He couldn't believe his mother went through such great lengths to hurt Abigail. In retrospect, Lady Darton owned that her behavior had been a bit extreme and even gave Dr. Fiske some monetary compensation for the trouble her actions had caused him.

Mrs. Locke grabbed another danish and leaned against Locke. The two were on a small couch in front of the fire. They could only stay Saturday and Sunday, whereas Abigail and Dr. Fiske had arrived at Darton on Friday and could remain until Monday. But Mrs. Locke said even just two days at Darton would be a wonderful stay for them. She seemed to be adjusting slowly but doing it well, just as Locke had complete confidence she would.

Walter raised an eyebrow. "How many of those have you had? The rest of us may want some."

Mrs. Locke waved a hand at him. "There's plenty. Dr. Fiske knows how I am and planned accordingly."

Dr. Fiske chuckled from the telescope. "We can set the other up," he said to Walter.

Walter nodded, and the two exchanged significant looks. *I want everything perfect.*

"Would you like a turn at the big scope, Lady Abigail?" asked Dr. Fiske several minutes later.

Abigail put down her spyglass and joined them.

Dr. Fiske walked towards the table and picked up the wine bottle. "We'll need another."

Abigail chuckled. "We do need to be lucid enough to identify what we're viewing."

Dr. Fiske laughed and set about the task of procuring another. Walter had several brought up from the cellar and had them put in the room next door.

Abigail gave a contented sigh. "What a marvelously clear night." She looked through the lens and jumped back. "What's this in the front?" She flipped the scope towards her so she could look at the lens.

"I thought I'd give you a different type of diamond."

Walter grinned. "One a little closer than the ones in the sky."

Abigail pulled the ring from the telescope and stared at it.

"Lady Abigail St. Clare, will you be my wife?" Walter asked.

Abigail gave a joyful gasp. "Yes, yes I will!" She jumped on him and threw her arms around his neck. "I absolutely will!"

Walter held her tight. *I'm never letting her go...*

"Walter, we're going to have such a wonderful life together," Abigail said. "We can do this all the time. And I can do your math, and we can—"

Walter gave her a kiss. "I love you, Abigail."

She smiled up at him. "I love you too."

Mrs. Locke whistled from the couch.

Abigail turned her head, her face flushed a pretty pink, but still grinning. "That was very unladylike."

"Good thing I'm not a lady," said Mrs. Locke.

Her husband pulled her closer. "You're my lady."

Dr. Fiske groaned, still holding an unopened bottle of wine. "You four aren't going to be like this all the time, right?"

"Dr. Fiske, I just got engaged." Walter beamed. "Where are your congratulations?"

"Congratulations." He smirked. "Again."

Mrs. Locke let out a peal of laughter.

Abigail gave her a look. "I'm about to relegate you to acquaintance status."

Mrs. Locke jumped up, still laughing, and rocked Abigail in a huge hug.

Epilogue

Eleven Years later

Walter

"Abigail! What is keeping you?" Walter asked, exasperated, as he entered her dressing room. "The guests are asking for you."

"I'm sorry. I got caught up with the equations, and the time got away from me." Abigail patted her hair while looking towards the mirror.

I wish she could wear it down. "You look beautiful as always. Just come."

"Is Teddy—"

"Teddy is fine. He's with the nurse."

"And Erwina is—"

"With the nanny along with Robert. The children are fine." Walter grabbed Abigail's hand and pulled her from her vanity chair. " I don't know how Mother has done it, but she's managed to collect some great scientific minds down there." He grinned at her. "The Herschels are here."

Abigail froze. "Miss Caroline Herschel too?"

Walter nodded, his smile growing wider.

Abigail squealed as her lovely gray eyes lit up.

The Dowager Darton, being the force she was recognized for in their society, did an about-face. Deciding she would try to help Abigail do what she had not been able, she became a staunch supporter of their research. This was one of many gatherings Walter's mother had put together for the discussion of science, and it appeared to be one of the best yet. She had even cautiously renewed her interest in chemistry. Walter was glad for that as it seemed to settle her and give her more peace.

Abigail was writing a mathematics book. She had decided to compile all the math lessons she had put together for Walter into a primer of sorts for others.

"Did you write to accept the invitation to Duke Hartwell's house party?" Walter asked as they walked down the stairs. Lord Manton had inherited his dukedom several years ago.

"I did," Abigail replied. "We'll have to decide what to do with the children as I believe the house party is adults only."

Walter squeezed her hand. "I don't mind that at all."

Walter and Abigail had less time for research with the children. Teddy was only a year and required a lot of attention and appeared to have Walter's looks. Robert was seven, and Erwina was five, and they resembled their mother. The nanny and nurse helped, but Walter and Abigail insisted on being with the children often. They spent many nights stargazing together — a family of amateur astronomers. Walter grinned. *Father would have been proud.*

*****

Abigail

The afternoon sped by.

A gentleman Abigail didn't know well but recognized as someone who coordinated conferences and lectures approached them. "We'd like to invite the two of you to speak at the next meeting of The International Astronomical League."

Abigail stilled. *Does he mean me too?* As Dr. Fiske had predicted, collaborating with him and Walter did get her notice. To the extent that other astronomers and scientists have asked for her input and assistance. *But to speak at a lecture would be extraordinary.*

Walter and her exchanged looks.

"Both of us?" Walter asked him.

The gentleman nodded. "Yes." He chuckled. "We'd like to hear an explanation of the mathematics that makes sense, Lord Darton."

Abigail smiled as her heart swelled with the compliment and anticipation for the opportunity.

Walter laughed. "Then yes, you most definitely need my wife." He glanced at her raising his eyebrows and grinning.

Abigail nodded vigorously, trying not to appear as though she were a child in a candy shop.

"We would be delighted," Walter said to the gentleman.

"Excellent. I'll write you the details."

Abigail stared after him as he walked away. "Both of us," she whispered.

Walter leaned down and kissed her cheek. "I'll be scandalous and kiss you in public."

Abigail giggled.

"Of course, he asked both of us," Walter said. "I can't go on without my partner, can I?"

Partners. In every way. Just like he said so long ago.

She beamed at him. "Neither can I, my love."

<<<>>>

an orphan
a fortune
a choice

When Hannah Northrop arrives at Archer Hall as the new governess, she doesn't have high hopes for being happy with the Barclay family. She never understood why her guardian, Lord Putnam, kept her in an orphanage for fifteen years only to bring her to his estate now when she's twenty years of age. All Hannah has ever wanted was a place. A family.

Kenneth Barclay wants a place as well, and he's just as convinced as Hannah that it's not at Archer Hall. Always at odds with his father, Lord Putnam, he's searching for an escape. But Kenneth is the heir, so he'll have to find a way to make do...

Oliver Vaughan has deep roots as the earl of his large estate, but he'll soon lose the last piece he regards as family. He's on a mission to ensure that Lady Corwyn's legacy remains.

Their lives are about to collide in a way that will leave them forever changed.

The following is an excerpt from
Who Is Madalene?-
The Women of T.H.E.T.A. Book 2: Hannah

PROLOGUE

MISS TERESA BARCLAY PUSHED her stepmother's wheelchair through the gardens of their estate. The doctor had told them her stepmother's heart was about to give out, so she must remain calm and comfortable because there was nothing more he could do for her. Teresa had difficulty comprehending that reality as Lady Putnam didn't appear gravely ill. Her black hair was still long and thick, and her dark eyes were vibrant.

"Teresa, I asked you to take a turn with me because I have an important request regarding a delicate situation."

They had a good relationship, but Teresa had never considered them close, so her stepmother's words took her by surprise. "What do you need? I'll help in any way I can."

Lady Putnam grabbed her hand. "Promise you'll do something for my niece, Hannah."

Teresa nodded. "I'll find a way to bring her here."

Relaxing, her stepmother sat back in the wheelchair and gently squeezed her hand. "Good. You have a way of getting things done, and your father minds what you say. He's not the man he may seem."

Teresa loved her father, but he wasn't the easiest of men to get along with. Yet, his marriage to Lady Putnam seemed to be one of love on both sides. News of her imminent death made him inconsolable.

"We were something, an important family," Lady Putnam said.

"Of course," agreed Teresa. "You married a viscount. You did very well."

Lady Putnam's connections were vague. She'd inherited a decent piece of property, but at the same time, her family hadn't lived the life of landed gentry. Hannah was her sole surviving relative.

Lady Putnam shook her head violently. "No, we were important, and it's gotten lost. You must bring back Hannah."

CHAPTER 1

Searching

Hannah

"MISS NORTHROP." The headmistress of the orphanage in Bath stood at the door of the classroom.

The children sat on benches in rows, the room darker than usual due to the clouds outside. The one dusty window didn't allow an extraordinary amount of light into the space.

Hannah Northrop told the student she was assisting to continue writing their consonants. She smoothed her black hair into the tight bun as she crossed the room, the floorboards creaking beneath her, and then curtsied before the headmistress. "How may I be of assistance?"

"Follow me to my office, Hannah," the headmistress replied. "I have something I'd like to discuss with you."

Hannah's blue eyes widened as she swallowed. *What could be wrong?* The children were rarely asked to come to the office, and when they were, it was usually due to an infraction. Every once in a great while, a fortunate child may be adopted. But Hannah had given up hope for that long ago — she was far too old as a twenty-year-old assistant teacher at the orphanage where she'd grown up. She willed the butterflies in her stomach to land as she stood in front of the desk.

The headmistress handed her an envelope. "This is payment from the milliner shop owner for the latest jingle you wrote."

Hannah pocketed the payment. She'd been creating advertisements and jingles for a few small shops in town. They didn't pay much, but it was something, and she enjoyed writing them.

"I've received a request from Miss Barclay," the headmistress continued.

Hannah raised an eyebrow. Miss Barclay was her late aunt's stepdaughter.

"She offers you an excellent position as a governess with the family at Archer Hall," said the headmistress.

Hannah was quiet a moment as she wasn't sure if this news should please or anger her. Her aunt's family brought a ready mix of volatile emotions.

The headmistress's eyes pinned her. "You need to accept this offer."

Silence filled the room as Hannah weighed her options and considered how she should answer. "I'm surprised and thankful for the offer of employment. But is there a reason why I'm not given a choice in this particular matter?"

"Payments for your upkeep will cease since this offer has been extended to you. The orphanage can no longer justify keeping your place since we already have several instructors."

Hannah's heart thudded. *My place was never permanent here and could've been halted at any time by my faceless guardian. It's a wonder this day hasn't come sooner.* "I understand. Thank you for informing me. I'll accept the offer directly and make immediate preparations to leave."

"Very good. I wish you well in your new life."

"Thank you." *I'll need it.*

*****

Kenneth

Mr. Kenneth Barclay stormed out of his father's study.

Lair. His evil lair.

Another meeting with his father, Percival Barclay, the Viscount of Putnam. *Father is far too heavy-handed with business.* Kenneth scowled. *With people.*

He thundered up the stone stairs to his quarters in Archer Hall, the sound reverberating in the large space. Once again, he was the one sent to deliver the message instead of his father. *The messenger boy— that's all Father sees me as. Twenty-five years old, and I'm still fetching and carrying like I'm twelve.*

Kenneth intercepted his manservant in the corridor. "Inform the stable master to ready my horse for immediate departure."

"Yes, sir. Might I remind you dinner will be served shortly."

"I won't be in attendance. I need—" Kenneth stopped short. If he stayed the night and left in the morning, he could finish the ship plan alterations and visit the builder while in London. At least that would give him a task of his own control of which to look forward.

I want to leave. Kenneth rubbed his face. *Trapped. I need to find my place.*

"I can arrange for dinner to be brought to your study," said his manservant.

He had probably heard the argument. Not that spats were an uncommon occurrence; Kenneth and his father rarely saw eye to eye.

"Do that," Kenneth replied. "I'll be a couple weeks in London and will send the address in case I need to be contacted."

"Very good, sir."

Kenneth continued down the corridor glancing out a window. It had been a chilly, dreary day and the remoteness of Archer Hall's surroundings stared back at him as the forests in the distance were eclipsed by darkness.

He slammed the door to his own study, threw himself into his chair, and shut his eyes. *What if I walked out of Archer Hall and never came back? Start fresh on my own?*

He exhaled. *I can't. I'm heir to Putnam, and I need to shoulder that responsibility.*

That's my place, whether I like it or not.

*****

Oliver

Oliver Vaughan, Earl of Vaughnryd, entered the secondary drawing room he and Lady Corwyn had dubbed the Project Heir room at her home in Derbyshire. Books, charts, and papers were strewn all over the place. A fire gave the room warmth and light, though the wall of windows on the east side allowed for plenty of sunshine to pour in.

He kissed Lady Corwyn's paper-thin cheek and frowned. *She's getting more fragile by the day.*

Her light blue eyes beamed at him. "You have the records I wanted. Dependable, smart boy." She patted his cheek. "Handsome too. Beautiful hazel eyes and all that dark hair. What are the ladies about these days? One should've snatched you up by now."

Oliver shook his head. His lack of lady was becoming a weekly topic of discussion. "How was your doctor's visit?"

"I'm fit as a fiddle."

"Lady Corwyn," he gently chided.

She pressed her lips into a thin line. "We need to find my heir now."

Grace Northrup, Countess of Corwyn in her own right, was his nearest neighbor and practically family. His only family left. Oliver dreaded the time when she'll leave him as well. He had deep roots here but wouldn't be connected to anyone.

"Come, child," Lady Corwyn said gently. "Let's get to work and see what you've found."

Oliver smiled. He would always be a child to her, even though he was a grown man of twenty-six.

"Have you a new lady?" she asked.

Oliver chuckled. "Not since you asked last week."

"You're right to be choosy — no sense in marrying poorly and messing up the works. But if you wait too long, you'll be doing this as well."

Lady Corwyn was searching for someone to bequeath her massive inheritance and titles. And she was right; he'll need an heir for his estate, Vaughnryd. They might be closing in on one for her, but there was confusion in the last two to three generations. Too many people had the same or similar names, and the surname had changed spelling.

Hopefully, these documents would help sort matters out.

The Women of T.H.E.T.A. series

Amid the British Industrial Revolution, players are taking their positions, and new battles are beginning — between individuals and within families, companies and industries, generations and their ideals. Relationships and loves are lost, old ones galvanized, and new ones forged.
Modern heroines
Unconventional heroes
Meet the women of T.H.E.T.A.

T.H.E.T.A. Books

Expanding Their Scope - The Women of T.H.E.T.A. Book 1: Abigail
Who Is Madalene? - The Women of T.H.E.T.A. Book 2: Hannah
The Hunt - The Women of T.H.E.T.A. Book 3: Rebecca
Sculpting His Likeness - The Women of T.H.E.T.A. Book 4: Faye
Forge - The Women of T.H.E.T.A. Book 5: Orelia

T.H.E.T.A. Novellas

The Foreman - The Women of T.H.E.T.A. Novella: Christiana (prequel)
The Imagination Room - The Women of T.H.E.T.A. Novella: Deanna (A Dr. Fiske story)

Future T.H.E.T.A. Books

The Ruins - The Women of T.H.E.T.A. Book 6: Mrs. Locke
TBD - The Women of T.H.E.T.A. Book 7: Jocelyn
TBD - The Women of T.H.E.T.A. Book 8: Portia

C.E.J., writing as Elizabeth Borae, resides in Pennsylvania, U.S.A. Besides writing, she has also worked as a literacy and mathematics tutor, specializing in working with children who have learning challenges. With a B.A. from Rutgers University majoring in Economics and Art History, she attempts to inject a little business into her stories about relationships and family during a period she loves in art and literature, the 19th century.